Robyn Davidson was born on 6 September 1950 in the Queensland town of Miles. Her journey by camel through Australia's interior was published to worldwide acclaim as *Tracks* (1980). She has published travel articles and autobiographical essays in many leading newspapers and magazines, and these are the basis for *Travelling Light*. She currently divides her time among London, New York and Alice Springs.

travelling
light

An imprint of HarperCollins*Publishers*

An Angus & Robertson Publication

Angus&Robertson, an imprint of
HarperCollins*Publishers*
25 Ryde Road, Pymble, Sydney, NSW 2073, Australia
31 View Road, Glenfield, Auckland 10, New Zealand

First published in Australia by William Collins Pty Ltd in 1989
Reprinted in 1989
This A&R revised Imprint Travel edition published in 1993
Reprinted in 1993

National Library of Australia
Cataloguing-in-Publication data:

Davidson, Robyn, 1950 –   .
   Travelling light.
   ISBN 0 207 18034 2.
   1. Davidson, Robyn, 1950 –   . Journeys.
   2. Voyages and travels – 1951. I. Title. (Series: Imprint travel)
910.40924

Cover photograph: detail from
Dee after she crossed the desert by William Yang
Printed in Australia by Griffin Paperbacks, Adelaide

9 8 7 6 5 4 3 2
97 96 95 94 93

'To keep the earth on one's roots and find another earth,
that is a real miracle.'

MARC CHAGALL

ACKNOWLEDGMENTS

Some of these articles have been published previously in a different form in the following newspapers and magazines: the *Sydney Morning Herald*, the *Age*, *Women's Day*, London *Sunday Times*, the *National Times*. 'The Mythological Crucible' was first published in *Australia, Beyond the Dreamtime* (Heinemann/BBC, 1987) as a slightly different version; 'Alice Springs' was first published by Collins Publishers Australia in 1989.

CONTENTS

THE MYTHOLOGICAL
CRUCIBLE

The Mythological Crucible

I was born in 1950 in the one-horse hospital of Miles, our nearest town, twenty-five miles away. It was a good year for Virgos, Robyns, and wars both hot and cold. The bumper crop of September births is easy enough to explain. The deprivations of the Pacific war were beginning to fade from memory, and there was enough money around not only to send care packages to England (a country my forbears had not seen for several generations but which some of them continued to call 'home'), but also to lash out on enough cold beer around the Yuletide season to forget about the importance of contraception. The burgeoning quantity of Robyns born in that decade remains a mystery.

At about the time I was being conceived, and myxomatosis was being introduced to exterminate the rabbit plague nibbling away at the roots of Australia's economy, a new government was being sworn in, to replace the Labor government which had seen Australia through the final years of the war. It was led by a bushy-eyebrowed man who rode to power on the promise of exterminating the Communist Party, which, according to him, was also decimating Australia's economy. It began what is known to history as the Menzies Era—sixteen years of it followed by a further seven years of conservative rule—the Big Sleep. According to my parents he was a shining statesman and a witty speaker. He was the good shepherd, who coaxed his bleating public into the safe pastures of economic prosperity and protected it from the dingo-like ravages of the Yellow Peril. He loved the Queen. He loved cricket. He was, above all, safe. There are other interpretations however. As an acquaintance of mine put it recently: 'Menzies was a poisonous old fart, hanging around the backside of Great Britain.' As the word 'fart' had never been heard in our household, I adhered, in my youth, to my parents' view.

We lived, my mother, father, sister and I, on a small—by Queensland standards—cattle property called Stanley Park. Even then the name seemed inappropriate to me. Parks were things which existed in places called London or Europe and they had oak trees and daffodils, fairies and Peter Pan. Rarely did we receive enough rain to turn the yellows and ochres of the Downs country into a poor excuse for green, or to send a muddy torrent choked with topsoil, bloated cattle and torn-up river gums down the wide, white creek bed which passed beside our house. It was one such torrent which almost carried our house away, and caused my father to sit on the front steps with his head in his hands, contemplating his losing battle with the bush and the bank. For we children, the thunderstorm was the most thrilling event in our lives. Hail lay a foot thick where once there had been dry grass and bluebells. Joyously we filled buckets with these miracles of ice, while our parents discussed 'selling up'.

Although I left Stanley Park when I was four, I remember, like a taste or a smell, a forlorn, deserted quality the country had. It was as if loneliness seeped out of the soil into the bright, brazen light. But of course that was a projection on my part, brought about, perhaps, by a guilty race conscience. Not far from where we lived a group of blacks had been murdered in a dry river bed fifty years before—a common enough occurrence during the dark ages of Australian history, which began in 1788 and continued until 1928, when the last recorded massacre of Aboriginal families took place. So carefully had my antecedents obliterated history that I knew nothing of this at the time. It would be many years before I discovered the rot which riddled white Australia's history, beneath the evasions, silences and lies, and longer still before an Australian prime minister would say: 'More than any foreign aid programme, more than any international obligation we meet or forfeit, more than any part we may play in any treaty or alliance, Australia's treatment of her Aboriginal people will be the thing upon which the rest of the world will judge Australia and Australians—not just now, but in the greater perspective of history.'

Our house was a typical bush homestead—rambling, ramshackle and set up on stilts to keep it cool. A succession of blue cattle dogs was chained up under the tank stand. A hardy variety of bougainvillea blazed along the peeling weatherboard walls; welcome swallows made their homes under the corrugated iron roof; deadly snakes made theirs in the woodpile. A succession of black and white cats prowled a wide veranda gauzed in by a fine wire mesh which, while effectively shutting out most of the relieving breezes of sundown, was no match for the squadrons of insects that kamikazed by the million each night into the hurricane lamps. It was these kinds of domestic difficulties— the spiders' webs, the dust, the piles of desiccating insects, the stray snakes and the lack of those modern appliances like vacuum cleaners and electric irons that littered the kitchens of her city chums—which caused my mother to sit on the back steps with her head in her hands.

Or perhaps it was the isolation that got her down. Her view, from those back steps, was of never-ending sameness. A solemn, empty, dry flatness with no distant mountains, no dazzling streams, no rich greens to relieve the eye. Yellows, sepias, drab bluey-greys stretched away to meet the empty blue vault, which bleached out as the day progressed and the sun crushed the vitality out of everything. One hundred years before, the explorer Ludwig Leichhardt—hero of Patrick White's novel *Voss*—passed across our land on his second attempt to cross Australia from east to west. He carved a large 'L' into a tree up in our brigalow forest before disappearing forever into the same oblivion as that which yawned before my mother's eyes. She was a city woman, used to an exciting social life. In her youth she had sung in operas, dressed herself up in chiffon and flowers and danced like Isadora Duncan. Oddly, my strongest image of her comes from a time before my birth. She described to me how, as a young woman, she had gone on a picnic with friends, and they had all decorated each other and the car with wild flowers. There were very few wild flowers at Stanley Park.

Our nearest neighbour lived three miles away. Our closest link with Elsewhere was the siding at Gulugaba—a tin shed beside the railway line. At the end of the long, rutted track in front of our house was a tin box on a stump, into which, once a week, were placed letters full of news and tacit sympathy from my mother's coast-clinging relatives: she was grateful for both. The wireless was our only other contact with the faraway world of events. Sometimes the cicadas and crickets were so loud that we had to turn it up to hear our favourite children's programme, 'The Argonauts', or our favourite serial, 'Blue Hills', or the Sunday play. When it came to news time my father moved his chair closer, cupped his hand over a war-damaged ear, puffed on his pipe and listened avidly. He may well have heard Menzies proclaim:

> The world is full of danger . . . China which we perhaps once regarded as an ancient and inactive country is in course of becoming a great power under the sternest Communist control. It seeks to expand, to divide and to conquer . . . Does any Australian sensibly believe that the defence of Australia's existence (because existence as a free country is what matters) would not be challenged if the Communists overran South-East Asia, subverted Indonesia and stood at the very threshold of our northern door?
>
> The simple English of this matter is that with our vast territory and our small population we cannot survive a surging Communist challenge from abroad except by the cooperation of powerful friends . . .

Twenty-five years later I would discover that, in the most remote areas of Australia, graziers were still preparing themselves for imminent invasion by little yellow people from the north. There was a drought on at the time, and the owners of cattle stations were hopping into their private Cessnas to fly to Canberra and demand drought relief. One of the reasons they gave to Parliament was that, if they had to walk off their properties, there would be no one left in the desert areas to defend the country against the Chinese. The idea that one gallant little family a hundred miles away from the next gallant little family could, by firing off their shotguns at the hordes emerging from the heat mirage along the horizon, save Australia from Communist takeover, might have been funny, if the gallant little families had not taken it so seriously.

Australians were obsessed with making money. They were fed up with the controls imposed by the war, with the growing number of civil servants in the federal capital, and with the strikers who, having suffered through the Depression and a war, wanted their share of the cake. Menzies had already proved himself a champion of war: in 1948, the year before he came to power, he had suggested the use of nuclear weapons to break the Berlin blockade. Then, in 1951, he announced that Australia would be at war again within three years. He was to send troops to Malaya and Borneo and, of course, to Vietnam. And in the year of my birth he committed Australia's armed forces to the great ideological conflict in Korea, in which Australia suffered nearly two thousand casualties. His Communist Party Dissolution Act was disallowed by the High Court in 1950, but the following year he attempted to obtain, by referendum, powers to deal with the Communists and to alter the Conciliation and Arbitration Act. The referendum was narrowly defeated, after a campaign in favour of political liberty by the leader of the opposition, H. V. Evatt. I do not know how my parents voted. I do know that to them, and to most people like them, Communism had replaced Fascism as the great world evil, and it was poised to take over Australia.

Every night when the news was over my father was available for bedtime stories. My sister and I sat beside him listening, enthralled, to tales of distant and romantic Africa, neither of us imagining that we too lived in a distant and romantic land. While my mother had been surviving the Depression my father had been wandering around the Dark Continent in a pith helmet, mining for gold, going on safari and, I suspect, poaching a bit of ivory. My strongest image of him comes from two

15

photographs—in one of them he is wading through waist-deep muddy water, holding a harpoon in his hand; in the next he is standing with his foot on the back of an enormous crocodile. He would speak of Africa wistfully, and perhaps it was because both my parents yearned to be somewhere else that I grew up restless and uncertain of where my home was. For despite the domesticity and hard work which rooted us to the various places in which we lived, they all had a temporary quality, as if we were waiting on the outskirts of something to which we would eventually belong. Or perhaps that is how many white Australians feel, like transplants who haven't quite taken root.

My parents' marriage was mixed: that is, she was urban, he rural. She was from the aspiring lower-middle class, which took pains to cover up any convict ancestry. He was from the landed squattocracy, which took pride in a non-convict ancestry. The love affair was legalised during the romance of war, and their wedding photo shows a deliriously happy couple—he in sergeant's uniform, she in tasteful crepe suit and a net fascinator which did not obscure the light of adoration in her eyes. I can well understand the attraction. She was all daintiness and grace and bubbling wit. He was all Errol Flynn. He was forty when they married; she was twenty-four. He had sailed back from Africa in a thirty-six-foot schooner and his eyes were the colour of the sea. Such is the stuff of grand passion.

But the stultifying niceness, the snug conservatism and the grasping materialism of the fifties left little room for that kind of romance. Excitement and adventure gave way to settling down, growing prosperous and raising publicly happy nuclear families even if it killed you. After the intensity of war, life must sometimes seem pallid to those who survived it. No doubt there were many people who felt, but could not explain, a certain hollowness in their lives which even the advent of swizzle sticks, plastic roses and lightweight irons could not fill.

Children somehow construct the truth out of whispers and secrets. Just as I could feel the undercurrents of discontent which ran beneath the wholesomeness of family life, so could I smell

16

the acrid remains of war, like smoke from a spent bush fire. The rare growling of a DC3 overhead would send me scuttling under the house to escape the bombs which must inevitably fall. And there were other, more subtle, anxieties. My father was almost a dead war hero. A friend of his, Ivan Lyon, had led a small group of hand-picked men into a Japanese harbour in the dead of night to place bombs on the hulls of enemy ships. The success of their mission demanded a repeat run. He contacted my father, who was eager to go but, being fortyish and having suffered two hernias already, not to mention blackwater fever, was regretfully deemed physically unfit. Ivan and all his crew were captured and beheaded by the Japanese. 'Who—and, for that matter, where—would I be,' I often thought, 'if Poppy had died in the war?' When old age had made him wise, his reminiscences of war heroism changed dramatically. Once, he described his shelling of a tank in Tobruk. A soldier had come out of the tank on fire. 'A human torch,' said my father, quickly blinking away tears. His fondest memory was of drinking beer with enemy Italians on Christmas Day. But, during my childhood, Jerries and Japs were the bad guys and war seemed like a game.

My mother's patriotic fervour manifested itself in a horror at the Japanese products which were beginning to flood the market. With pursed and disapproving lips she would check the bottoms of cups to see if they bore that terrible brand 'Made in Japan'. The same disapproval was reserved for some German neighbours of ours, who had been interned during the war years and were still unpopular in the community. Whether they were Nazi sympathisers or not, their guttural accents would ensure that they remained unpopular long after Japanese gadgets became ideologically desirable. Japan, after all, was soon to become a major buffer zone against the Communists. But bitter though my mother may have been towards the enemy, she did not gloss over the devastations of war. 'Their faces were green, pea green,' she once whispered. She was describing corpse-like American soldiers returning from the Pacific, marching through the streets of her home town.

It is not surprising that an emotional dulling, a deadening of the imagination, like shell shock, pervaded the post-war decade. Australia had seen the world and become linked to its fate, and the fate of the world was in question. I was two years old when the wind changed direction off the Monte Bello Islands and blew radioactive material from Britain's first nuclear bomb across the Australian continent.

Like most women of the fifties, my mother was not immune to the barrage of propaganda designed to get females out of the workforce and back into the home. They had done their duty for the war effort by occupying the vacuum left by the fighting men and entering the world of production. Now their duty was to dismount graciously from their tractors and get on with the proper business of reproduction. Women's magazines were crammed with stories of selfless housewives giving up their talents, their passions, their ambitions for the sake of love, marriage, family. Recently I re-read a batch of them, and the propaganda is so blatant that it is difficult to believe that women of the time were not conscious of being manipulated. One story which particularly struck me was that of a woman artist who decides to enter a painting in a competition. She knows that it is her best work yet, and that she is sure to win. But her creative effort takes time away from her husband, who becomes sulky and morose. In the end she throws the painting in a puddle, and as she watches the colours dribble down the canvas she feels an enormous relief and a sudden joy. So, one imagines, does hubbie.

Contemporary Australia has a reputation for producing tough-minded women. Indeed, tough-minded women are one of our principal exports. In a culture whose misogyny has deep historical roots, and in which women were traditionally regarded as something like a cross between a sheep and a kitchen appliance, it is only to be expected that daughters of fifties' mothers should have produced an antipodean feminism with a sharp cutting edge.

White women were not the only ones shuffled up and down the economic ladder by the vagaries of war. While Aborigines in Western Australia were being prevented from moving south of the twentieth parallel (the 'leper line'), and still others were being gaoled as 'potential enemies', some of their more fortunate relations in the centre and the north were being employed on war construction projects. They did not yet have the vote, but for the first time they did receive decent wages and housing. Aboriginal women, too, were brought from the forgotten settlements of the outback to work as domestics in the city—that is, to occupy those jobs which white women could now afford to vacate. Most of those black women had never seen a town, let alone a city. They were forced to leave family and country behind. Traumatic it may have been, but when the war ended so did six years of money and relative comfort. Many did not want to return to the bottom of the barrel. They had little choice.

My mother appeared to accept her post-war role without anger, fully expecting the happiness promised her by all the happy endings of all the stories in all the women's magazines. She became, in true Australian tradition, a civilising influence on rough and ready rural life.

She taught primary school lessons to my sister via the correspondence system. She was both nurse and doctor to us, because there were no nurses or doctors within cooee. She learned how to pull cattle from bogs, strain fencing wire, chop wood and be alone for days on end. On her treadle Singer she sewed dresses with ruffles, pintucks and puffed sleeves. She polished the cracked floorboards of the dining room until you could see your face in them. She dug a garden and coaxed silver beet, our staple green, out of the dry, unyielding earth. From the basics of weevilly flour, salt beef and sugar she brought forth culinary masterpieces of the strictly English type. On Mondays she washed everything by hand, rinsed it in Bluo and starched it, ready for Tuesday—the day for damping down, plonking irons on the top of the Kooka wood stove, and sweating over each flounce and tuck while the temperature climbed into the hundreds. She read us books, scrimped to buy us an encyclopaedia from a travelling salesman, and encouraged us to sing around the piano of a Saturday evening. She threaded ribbons in our hair, and lobbied our father for one or two train trips to that remote and unimaginable place, the city. She fed the lean, ragged, dried-up swagmen who still arrived at our door from time to time, looking for bit work or tucker. She learned to lie convincingly to the dodgy strangers who came and leered and asked if she were alone. 'My husband will be back directly,' she would say, holding the snarling dog by the collar.

But she never managed to overcome her snake phobia. Even getting to the dunny at night was an expedition fraught with danger. Tiger snakes, king browns, western browns and copperheads were too much for my mother's fertile imagination. Having negotiated the path with much beating of long grass and peering down with the lantern, there were still the redbacks hiding on the underside of the lid of the loo to contend with.

Life in the bush was full of such hazards. I was much too young to remember when our first car replaced the horse and dray. But I do dimly recall the day we drove the Austin through bush fires and my sister and I almost expired. Wet cloths were pressed to our skin as the flames along the side of the road cracked open gum trees as if they were penny fireworks.

That my family's bank balance was not rocketed into the black by the economic boom was not the fault of the boom. My father was an amateur astronomer, geologist and naturalist. He was a spinner of yarns, a talented craftsman and a dreamer. But his whimsical attitude to life, his gentleness and his deeply held Victorian values meant that he lacked the qualities needed for getting rich quick—chicanery, judgment and competitiveness. He also lacked luck. Wool prices were soaring; my father owned cattle. Minerals were being unearthed everywhere; my father neglected to buy shares. Like returning soldiers from the First World War, who had been given plots of barren land infested with mallee (if Gallipoli hadn't killed them, the mallee would), my father took up land which was choked with forests of brigalow. Without the capital with which to improve the property, hire labour or invest in one of the American tractors which were proliferating across the landscape like flies, his efforts at improvement were about as effective as scratching at a diamond. Off he would go before sun-up, with his stockwhip, dog and axe, his packed lunch, thermos of tea and the whistle of an optimist, to saddle his horse. At night he would come home reeking of sweat, pleased with an honest day's work, whereupon he would sit with his legs up and ruminate on the wonders of nature and the beauty and mystery of the stars, while my mother heated water on the Kooka for his bath, made restless tapping sounds with her fingers, and gave out exasperated little sighs. After his fourth strangulated hernia, the doctors said, 'Five and you're dead.'

'Load of bunkum,' said my father, smiling reassuringly through a barrage of exasperated sighs. He was to prove the doctors wrong.

The year 1954 was a very big one for us all. Previously, it seemed, nothing had ever changed. My dad's boots always sat by the front door. The yapping of the cattle dog and the clanking of corrugated iron in the wind were incessant. On Saturday, a boiled lolly was inevitably doled out by my mother's hand. Even when the bush fires came, or the hail made our house look like a Christmas card, even when my father lay doubled up with another hernia, or came home on his horse twice his normal size because he had ridden into a nest of wasps—even these momentous events were fixed in a bedrock of sameness. But in 1954 not only did the Queen pay her first visit to her Australian subjects, not only did the name Petrov strike fear and loathing into many Australian hearts, not only did the Labor Party begin to self-destruct, but the Davidson family crossed the aptly named Great Dividing Range, leaving the western slopes forever.

The long drive from Gulugaba to Mooloolah was undoubtedly hot, dusty and fraught with tensions, and I'm glad I don't remember it. What I do recall was standing pressed close to my mother in a very crowded street, waving a little flag at a big black car. A lady with a pretty hat was waving back. Books may not have been a big feature in many Australian homes at the time, but invariably, alongside the Bible and the Children's Encyclopaedia, there would be a pop-up picture book of the coronation. Mothers dreamed secretly that their daughters would get hitched to Prince

21

Charles. The Queen's hats were copied by milliners all over the country. Such intense royalism has left its mark in the subconscious of ordinary Australians. I know very few people who haven't dreamt that some member of the royal family visited them for a cuppa or a sexual encounter.

The Great Dividing Range runs all the way down the eastern coast of the continent, separating wet from dry, urban from outback, dense population from sparse. It also divides reality from myth, for, while the early settlers huddled along the thin strip of coast, looking longingly across the seas to the real world, it was the dry country, the open, empty spaces of the interior that white Australians, the most urbanised population in the world, chose as their mythological crucible—a place where mateship, masculinity, xenophobia and philistinism were mixed to form the old stereotype we know and dislike so well, and which does not, and never did, do justice to the complexity of that elusive, problematical thing, national identity.

The village of Mooloolah boasted an industrial centre (one sleepy sawmill), a shopping centre (one tiny post office which doubled as a general store) and a cultural centre (one Methodist church a bit bigger than the dunny at Stanley Park, one derelict School of Arts Hall, and a primary school in which two teachers taught anything from fifteen to forty pupils, depending on the weather). I suppose all of us in that little community were pioneers of a kind. There was no building in the area more than thirty years old. We were part of a new wave, doing what our ancestors had done before us in other parts of the country—clearing bushland and preparing it for an invasion of groundsel, prickly pear, lantana, bracken, Paterson's curse and Scotch thistles. It was the super-phosphates that gave the paddocks their sheen of English green.

Perhaps my mother thought, when she saw the lush kikuyu pastures of our new home, that her husband's business acumen had taken a turn for the better. A sign proclaiming 'Malabah' in bold letters swung from a high wooden gate, behind which stood the Big White House on the Hill. Away from the house rolled two hundred acres of emerald paddocks, laced with babbling brooks and dotted with trees that looked like trees, and with sheep. We were a mere sixty miles from Brisbane, and the Pacific beaches lay twelve miles to the east. There was electricity, an ox-heart mango tree, rampant alamanda vines and an inside lav. I know that, as far as my mother was concerned, 'Malabah' had one attribute that surpassed all others. Tiger snakes, copperheads, western browns and king browns all lived on the other side of the Great Divide.

'Can you tell me what Mooloolah means?' she asked vivaciously after introducing herself to the store owner and postmaster.

'Abo word. Means red-bellied black snake. Poisonous buggers.'

The place was riddled with them. They dangled from the rafters of my cubby house. They slithered through the floorboards of the laundry. They sunned themselves on the passionfruit vine. They entered my mother's nightmares. It would not be long before she would be sitting on the back steps of our new home with her head in her hands, muttering that 'Malabah' was nothing but a white elephant. It was such a poetic description of the solid, comfortable old house that at the time I could not understand her bitterness.

It is not quite correct to say that Australia rode on the sheep's back. It rode on the Merino's back. My father's unerring instinct for failure had led him to buy Romney Marsh and Border Leicester sheep. English sheep that found the steamy fecundity of the subtropics a less than ideal environment and that suffered from footrot, staggers, worm infestations, pink-eye, fly-blown rumps, tumours and the kind of stupidity that led them to die in large numbers during the floods and bush fires, or that enabled them to get themselves tangled up in the six-foot-high dingo-proof netting fences to which my father dedicated several more hernias and through which the wild dogs inevitably found their way.

There is a debate in Australia, between conservationists and farmers, concerning the eating habits of the native-born dingo. From my own experience I would say that a pure-bred dingo will rarely, if ever, attack a lamb. But domestic dogs who have gone feral, or dog–dingo crosses, will disembowel a whole flock for the sheer joy of it. We lost sixty of our two hundred sheep in one night. They lay scattered across the paddocks like bits of bloodied cottonwool. My father put them out of their misery with a bullet to the brain. The optimistic whistling and the exasperated sighs were back with a vengeance.

But, for all our money worries, we were rich in comparison with our neighbours, and our dilapidated three-bedroom house could only be seen as luxurious when compared to the one-room shacks in which many of the dairy farmers and their families lived. Their holdings were too small ever to make a profit, and their lives consisted of never-ending work just to make ends meet. The children would be up by four in the morning, bringing in the cows for milking. After school they would hurry home, sometimes many miles, on their ponies or on foot for more of the same. What was most astonishing to me was that many of the farmers did not speak English very well.

It is sometimes forgotten that Australia is a land of immigrants. If it has become chic to find a convict ancestor, it is because there just aren't that many. The gold rush of the previous century attracted the first great wave, increasing the population threefold. Between the end of the Second World War and the early seventies three million came. As with previous intakes, preference was given to the British, ninety per cent of whom received assisted passage. But during this period Europeans formed over half of the new arrivals.

Workers feared competition in the labour market. Protestants worried about an inundation of 'Micks'. Jews feared the arrival of Nazi sympathisers. Leftists were concerned at the conservatism of new arrivals who had suffered such trauma in Europe and who now wanted, above all, safety and stability. Menzies, who after the war continued Labor's policy of large-scale immigration, assured them of both. Previously there had been only Abos and Chinks for Anglo-Saxon Australians to feel superior to. Now there were Italians, Greeks, Poles, Yugoslavs, Finns—a smorgasbord for the xenophobe.

By the time we arrived in Mooloolah many of the new Australians had begun to spread out into country areas. Our closest neighbour and friend was a Pole. He owned a Land Rover and a small pineapple farm skirting the precipitous slopes of infertile hills. In all the time I knew him, Ted never quite managed to master the English language. But it didn't matter. We adored each other, and who needs conversation for that. He brought me freshly crushed pineapple juice, and when he smiled his whole face wrinkled up in a most delightful way. Later on, his wife arrived fresh as a rose from Scotland. Like my parents, they had met as a consequence of war and it had taken Ted several years to provide a home for her.

I remember quite clearly the day he finished building his shack ready for her arrival. It was simply the best cubby house I had ever seen—twenty foot square, with a neat double bed, a sink and a wood stove. Outside on the gritty white soil lay stacks of empty crates in which the pineapples would be sent south to the cannery. Beside them were mounds of pineapple tops, reeking and ready for planting. It is likely that Bunty regarded her new home with less enthusiasm than I. When Ted brought her to meet us she sat in the Land Rover with a dazed, uncomprehending look on her face, as if she had just landed on Mars. My mother's heart bled for her.

Bunty had skin that was almost transparent, and so soft it looked as if a powder puff would scratch it. The sandflies and mosquitoes smelt her Scottish blood a mile off and zoomed in for the kill. She could not resist scratching at the red welts which made her ankles and legs swell and then turn septic. In the height of summer they would both be out chipping the pines: that is, walking along the rows, hoeirg weeds—thousands of weeds, miles of rows. The serrated leaves of the pines scratched at Bunty's legs and arms and gave her tropical ulcers. The skin of her hands split and cracked and the acid juice stung and burned them.

What, I wonder, had she expected of the 'lucky country'? An exotic South Seas paradise, dripping with wealth, where the ravaged of the world could find peace at last? If so, her disillusionment must have been painful indeed. I sensed that her initial loathing of Australia was so profound that she could find no beauty in it anywhere. Often they came with us on one of our boring Sunday drives—a fifties' form of torture for children, who fought in the back seat of the Holden, got car-sick and vomited on the side of the road.

'Isn't this beautiful?' my mother said hopefully, encouragingly, sweeping her arm to indicate the primeval emptiness which folded away in every direction.

'Oo aye,' said Bunty, her lips compressing. It was not beautiful and it was not Scotland. Through her eyes I glimpsed what the first settlers must have seen, and understood how much they must have ached.

I do not know Ted's story, but I gleaned from the way my parents spoke that his sufferings during the war would have been inconceivable to people like us. And here he was, in the back blocks of nowhere, burning himself up—aware, no doubt, behind his shy smile, of the indifferent, faintly contemptuous attitude towards people like himself of the nation to which he now belonged.

Our neighbours on the other side were dairy farmers, and it wasn't just the threat of their crazed Jersey bull which made my mother caution us against crossing the boundary fence. There was an aura of mystery surrounding them, and I did not understand until later that it emanated from the kind of squalor abject poverty can produce. There must have been fourteen children, few of whom ever went to school. My father often grumbled that their fences needed mending, and when they came through our property they left the gates open and stole guavas. He shook his head ruefully, and pronounced them 'no-hopers'.

While the academic education provided by Mooloolah state school was virtually non-existent, there is one thing which must be said in its favour. Everyone, from upper-crust to hill-billy, had a turn at being the victim. Colour, race or class had little to do with the pecking order. Everyone was treated equally badly; everyone had at least one quality for which he or she could be teased, bullied and persecuted. A funny nose, a funny name, it didn't matter much. It was there in the playground that young Australians, old and new, learned the art of sniffing out and snuffing out difference of any kind and excellence in any form—except, perhaps, brute strength, where baby poppies learned to hack each other off at the stem as soon as they looked like growing tall. Schooldays were the incubation period for a national lack of self-esteem. To be 'up oneself', to be 'too big for one's boots', to be a 'smart Alec'—these were the commonest forms of abuse.

In the population at large this cultural inferiority complex, this surly defensiveness, manifested itself in an obsession with assimilation. Immigrants were tolerated if they ate our kind of food, believed in our values and learned how to cop insults with a self-deprecating grin. Nino Culotta, who wrote a book called *They're a Weird Mob*, was both comic and forgiving in his description of the mutual puzzlement of old Aussie and new. The book was very popular in the late fifties: white Australia liked the image of itself that he created. But what the book revealed was the fact that Australia was willing to accept immigrants only to the same degree to which the immigrants were willing to adapt, to assimilate. When 'otherness' could not, or would not, be disguised, when the skin was too black or the eyes too slanted, the more brutal forms of racism appeared.

But every cloud has a silver lining. It was in the playground that little Australians also developed their inbuilt bullshit detectors, their lack of undue reverence, their mistrust of elitism and their laconic, ironic, dry-creek-bed, self-flagellating wit. Australians will be the first to send themselves up, as if, expecting to be laughed at by the world, they can maintain a certain dignity by laughing at themselves first.

Gypsies have always frightened sedentary populations with their 'otherness', and it was no different in Mooloolah. They parked their wagons and grazed their horses on the field near the railway station, sharpened a few knives and scissors, then passed on. I don't think anyone ever said, 'Don't go near the tinkers' camp', but I somehow absorbed—from my family, from my teachers—

that it was not a wise thing to do. I deeply regret not having followed the dictates of my own curiosity. By the late fifties they had disappeared. Whether they withdrew from Australia, or were gradually absorbed into the dominant culture, I do not know. In either case, the great Australian drive towards homogeneity had won out.

That the great drive did not succeed, after two hundred years of sustained effort, in turning Aborigines into white men has everything to do with the resilience of Aboriginal culture, of which I had no inkling in my youth. Perhaps if there had been any Aboriginal families left in the area I might have received information different from that provided by the social studies books at school, which portrayed Aboriginal people as ignorant, barbaric creatures with dirty habits, inferior in all mental and spiritual processes to the white man, which was why their demise was inevitable. (This description is still being taught in primary schools, at least in Queensland.) But there were no Aborigines here. The survivors of disease and war had been rounded up and sent to government settlements which were, and often still are, concentration camps—out of sight, out of mind.

Tolerance was not one of Mooloolah's gifts to its children, but it was a wonderful place for the free development of the imagination. Without the restrictions of television and masses of toys, my sister and I constructed worlds out of dirt, sticks and pebbles and populated the countryside with fabulous creations. We were bursting with the vitality produced by a diet which was the best the earth could offer—fresh fish, every kind of fruit and vegetable, home-baked bread, milk straight from the udder, home-grown mutton. To those not initiated into the secrets of our games, Mooloolah might have seemed a dull place. To us, it was paradise.

I am still struck by the physicality and self-reliance of Australian children. They are more often than not riding surfboards by the time they are six, and producing skin cancers by the time they are twenty. With all that energy and weather, who could bear to be inside studying, or reading books, or practising the piano, or learning how to make polite conversation with grown-ups? My mother worried, therefore, that we might grow up without accomplishments. Once a fortnight we were taken to Nambour, our nearest town, to sit at the piano and have pennies placed on our wrists by nuns with rulers in their hands. Every three weeks three books would arrive by post, which I would have to pretend to read. One day my mother caught me out.

'Did you enjoy your book about Mozart?'

'Oh, yesss.'

'All right, then. What was his first name?' After a few moments of silence she pointed to the title spread right across the cover— *Wolfgang Amadeus Mozart*.

'I just forgot,' I said, and got whacked with the book.

If she's so anxious for me to read, I thought, how come she locks some books in a cupboard? *Lady Chatterley's Lover*, for example, and *Ulysses*.

She battled, too, to bring an appreciation of the higher things to the culturally deprived people of Mooloolah. Under her guiding hand, night-life flourished in the School of Arts Hall. Theatrical events were staged in which I featured heavily. In my time I have been both a Wattle Fairy (I was so *embarrassed* by those yellow bloomers) and Mary, Mother of Jesus. I have sung 'Life is Great in the Sunshine State' to audiences who cheered my high C. The older kids got to sing 'Tan Shoes and Pink Shoelaces'. I thought this was rather unfair, but took what parts were offered.

She scoured the district for women who could play the piano. While the men scattered Pops Dancing Dust on the floor the ladies took turns on stage, thumping out waltz tunes all in the same key. Men scrubbed up, slicked their hair down with Californian Poppy, and donned broad-lapelled suits if they had them, clean shirts and khaki trousers if they didn't. Women wore mid-length dresses with gathered skirts, and when they stepped out for the Pride of Erin or the progressive barn dance the men placed a handkerchief chivalrously against their partner's backs so as not to mark the pretty frocks. Alcohol was forbidden. Wooden seats borrowed from the school lined the four sides of the hall, one of which opened onto an annexe where tea in glass cups would be served at supper—along with the sandwiches, scones, pikelets and lamingtons that the ladies had made that afternoon. At 10 p.m. the dancing would end and supper would be called—children first, then adults. And while the adults were sipping their tea with little fingers outstretched, and yarning about weather and falling pineapple prices, the children would drag each other, horse-and-cart style, from one end of the slippery floor to the other.

But the excesses of Saturday night had to be paid for by the sobriety of Sunday mornings. Oh, how I loathed Sunday school. How I despaired of the fortnightly visits from the preacher, who maundered on and on and on like a blowfly, while our scalps itched under our white panama hats, and our knickers prickled under pastel nylon frocks, and our palms perspired onto our plastic purses which contained nothing other than a freshly ironed hanky and sixpence for the collection plate. Could there have been a worse torment than sitting in the heat, watching my dad embarrass my mum by dropping off in the pew and snoring, until the tattered little congregation burst forth with 'Bringing in the Sheep'?

Yes. Our increasingly frequent visits to the city. Now when I say 'city' I really mean large, sprawling country town, in which the most exciting shops were Myer's Emporium and Dalgety's Stock and Station Agents. Brisbane was a dreamy, languid place, a town of never-ending Sundays. Long, exhausting journeys on the train ended in a dose of cod liver oil from my grandmother, who would be waiting, spoon poised, at the other end. After recovering from that there would be baked dinner in a closed up pigeon-box house, its windows bolted and curtains drawn against the vulgarity of Australia's weather. Sweat dribbled silently onto the starched linen napkins which were tucked into our lace collars, while cricket commentary droned out of the radio and pigeons cooed in the neat backyards of an infinite suburbia, and nothing dangerous was said.

I think these visits were most difficult for my father, who, when released from the cramped confines of the interior, would look out over the rapidly spreading suburbs of fibro and weatherboard, and reminisce about the time when all this had been a paper-bark swamp: 'I used to hunt black duck here when I was a boy. The creeks were fresh and clean, full of fish. There used to be white sandbanks in the Brisbane River. But you've got to have progress.'

The decade was coming to an end, and so were my sister's utopian days. Puberty struck, and whatever else may be said in Mooloolah's favour its teenage social life was not exactly swinging. My pain at her disappearance into adulthood and boarding school was somewhat alleviated by the advent of television. When we made our fortnightly visits to Nambour these days we would see knots of people crowded around shop windows, their blank faces flickering in the spectral lights of the magic box. When the stationmaster bought a set we began having social evenings at his house, during which we greatly admired the twenty-six-inch screen sitting inside a rosewood veneer cabinet with legs, and sang along with the advertising jingles. The pressure on my father was enormous, and at last he caved in.

The modern era moved into our lounge room and set about destroying conversation, sing-songs around the piano and our addiction to radio. Previously, our best outing had been going to the Eudlo cinema of a Friday night. (The cinema was a converted School of Arts Hall.) We would pack the ute with blankets and thermoses of coffee and head off into the twilight. On the way home I would sleep in the back, under the stars, while my dad swerved to avoid marsupials along twelve miles of gravel road.

But now our Eudlo adventures were abandoned, along with my timeless afternoons. No longer did I hang around the store with Jennifer Garbutt and Susan Turner, swapping penny lollies after school. No longer did I collect botanical specimens and dead insects for my scrapbooks, or spend hours on the swing, composing symphonies and poems. No longer did I race down to the paddocks to 'help' my father with the shearing/dipping/drenching/milking, and to listen to him talk about infinity and

31

other great matters. Now it was home lickety-split to grab a Vegemite sandwich and join in the singing of 'M-I-C-K-E-Y M-O-U-S-E' with a pair of black plastic ears stuck on my head.

In 1959 my mother became ill and we decided to join the ever-increasing surge of people leaving country areas for the towns and cities, where doctors and jobs were prevalent. Perhaps the decision had as much to do with our failure to make money out of 'Malabah', but whatever the cause the move marked a profound change for all of us. My father entered an uneasy retirement; my mother, a deep depression. And I'm sure my own blanking out of the early sixties had much to do with massive culture shock.

With the sale of 'Malabah' my father had made his last financial blunder. Not too many years later our Mooloolah neighbours would cash in on the land boom and sell their dairy farms to coastal developers for fabulous sums. Later still the hippies would arrive, fresh from the revelations of the Asian trail and with enough wealth behind them to choose poverty as a way of life. They built ashrams and geodesic domes and planted dope where once impoverished dirt-farmers had scratched to earn a living. I have not been back, but I hear that 'Malabah's' sheep have been replaced by quickly replicating brick veneer houses with exposed aggregate gardens and mock Roman columns. And the wild beaches and the wallum country behind them are now crowded with high-rise developments. Paradise lost.

If life in the country in the fifties meant isolation, in the suburbs it meant loneliness. Here we were, surrounded by an ocean of houses, but where was the community? What would take the place of the dances in the School of Arts Hall, or the kinds of bonds created between men and women when they set out together with their hessian sacks to fight the bush fires? In the kitchen we had an electric stove, a fridge and a Mixmaster. We had a vacuum cleaner and a floor polisher. On Sundays it was the whirring of Victa lawn-mowers that woke us up rather than the chorus of songbirds. We had a television that cost £250 and more time than we had ever had before in which to do nothing. Which is mostly what we did.

My father twiddled his thumbs and dug the garden. Some days he went fishing for flathead in the estuary, but it wasn't much fun alone. My mother stared out of windows a great deal and took handfuls of Bex powders with tonic water. We all spent a lot of time watching 'I Love Lucy', 'Perry Mason', 'The Cisco Kid', '77 Sunset Strip', 'Liberace' and 'Pick-a-Box' on television. My sister, five years older and more worldly than me, watched 'Bandstand' and 'Six O'clock Rock' during her infrequent visits home from school. I spent most of my time strolling across the golf course which bordered our house, worrying about just what it was that went on behind the lavatories at my new school. In Mooloolah there had been thirty pupils in the whole school. Now there were thirty in my class. Thirty children who rode bicycles rather than horses and knew all about sex.

I read somewhere recently an argument for suburban living. 'It reconciles access to work and city with private, adaptable, self-expressive living space at home. Plenty of adults love that living space, and subdivide it ingeniously. For children it really has no rivals.' I suspect that the man who wrote it had not spent time in places like Redcliffe. Perhaps my loneliness would have been assuaged if I'd joined in the throbbing social life centred around Redcliffe's cinema. But my mother was over-protective and, besides, the cinema was the meeting ground for those purveyors of decadent values, the Bodgies and Widgies, who offended social *mores* by going in for unconventional fashion—stovepipe trousers did not conceal Presley purple socks. The Widgies lolled on the backs of their Bodgies' bikes, jingling razor-blade bracelets.

To my parents, these rebels without a cause were a symbol of everything that was going wrong in the world—the traditional values of hard work, puritanism and thrift, developed through first the Depression and then the war, were being mocked and undermined. Every Saturday night teams of these youngsters would ride their bikes up from Brisbane to hang around outside

33

hamburger shops, terrorising the sleepy residents of the backwater with the insolent way they sucked on their milkshakes.

My father believed that these 'juvenile delinquents' should be drafted into the army to make men of them. As for me, I was both frightened and fascinated. They were like butterflies with poisonous stings and they seemed to be having more fun than I was. Sometimes I was allowed to go to the Saturday matinée at the cinema with the older boys from next door. They had an F. J. Holden, they were reliable, and they didn't mind having a little kid along. There I discovered that the Bodgies' pranks were pretty tame—lots of whistling, lots of necking with Widgies up the back, lots of Jaffas being rolled down under the seats, but nothing dangerous. Alas, these Saturday outings were stopped when a more serious faction who mixed hard liquor with their milkshakes came into the theatre and ran up and down the aisles slashing the seats with flick-knives.

By the time my sister left school she was well on the way to becoming a wild one, but of the beatnik variety. My mother admonished her to buy cotton frocks and sensible shoes; she went in for black sloppy joes, white lipstick and Intimate perfume. She gave me cigarettes to smoke in the toilet when I was eleven, and hinted that there was life beyond Redcliffe. She was standing on the wrong side of the generation gap and I ached to join her, but I had my four-year stretch in boarding school to live through before I could take the leap.

We were seldom allowed to watch television at school, and never allowed to read newspapers. It was hinted, in our final year, that universities were places where doctors and lawyers went, but the prospective wives of doctors and lawyers did not. All sorts of social causes were claiming the youth of the country (forty per cent of the population was now under twenty-one), but the girls of St Margaret's School remained oblivious. The first sounds of mass radicalism on the streets did not penetrate the high walls of the grounds. Socialism was regarded as a kind of social leprosy. When Lyndon Baines Johnson visited Australia in 1966 our school organised a parade to line the streets and

34

wave, just as we had waved to the Queen in previous years. But the canon who took chapel that day stretched the service out with a sermon concerning the evils of war, thereby depriving us of the possibility of going 'all the way with L.B.J.'. 'That canon must be some kind of Pinko,' we all agreed.

My unfocused rebellion led me to skip classes and spend most of my time in the music rooms, thumping out passionate rhapsodies and practising for the day when I would fulfil my mother's dream and become a famous concert pianist. Consequently I received a scholarship to the Conservatorium of Music but missed out on one to the University. Music was, in fact, our one legitimised contact with the world outside. Every Saturday night we were allowed to play our records and practise jiving, twisting and surfie-stomping with each other, while the nuns' heads bobbed up and down to the beat of 'Bombora', 'Roll Over Beethoven' and 'Blue Gene'. There was much debate over which of the Beatles was the most desirable, and whether the Rolling Stones could ever match up. Another topic of conversation was how minuscule you could make your bikini and still stay within beach regulations. On one of my few holidays up the coast with a schoolfriend, my one-piece costume guaranteed wallflower status on the sands. Zinc-nosed surfies and life-savers just passed me by.

Shortly after Prime Minister Harold Holt vanished into the surf at Portsea, I vanished from the school arena. Like any released prisoner I had to learn what had happened to the world while I was 'inside'. I set about discovering the sixties. The country was wealthier than it had ever been, thanks to a mining boom reminiscent of the old gold rush days. But, despite this, Australia was experiencing an upheaval such as it had never had before. There were many issues over which dissension arose, but the main one was, of course, the conscription of young, voteless Australian men, by ballot, to fight in Vietnam. This was the state of the world I entered, and I joined the flood of demonstrators like a duck taking to water. I gave up my scholarship to the Conservatorium (the students there seemed to be fiddling while Rome burned) and began hanging around at Queensland

35

University, arguably the most radicalised campus in Australia. I got a job there which allowed me to attend courses free of charge at night—although I have to admit that academic education was not what I was after. I wanted to *live*.

When my father visited my commune, young men covered in unkempt hair did not get up to shake his hand. Women in army fatigues or see-through kaftans revealed bra-less chests. Posters of Lenin glowered down at two weeks worth of washing up stacked in the kitchen sink. But what he found really intolerable were the new words which peppered our language—words like 'fuck', 'fuckin' ' or 'fucked', as in 'Most people over forty are fucked.' My dear old dad was deaf to the answers that were blowing in the wind, and all he could see was the insufferable arrogance of a spoilt generation.

My visits to him were only slightly more satisfactory. 'Gawd, Rob,' he would say, as soon as I met him at the door, 'haven't you got a nice dress to wear?' Tersely I would assure him that I liked wearing men's bowling trousers, a jumper with holes in it, red patent leather boots and a beret. Within five minutes we would be arguing. I would accuse him of being an old reactionary, who didn't know what he was talking about. He would accuse me of being a silly young twerp. We were both right.

The overnight train journey from Brisbane to Sydney takes sixteen hours—plenty of time in which to wonder whether you are doing the right thing. The design of the seats renders comfort impossible in any position. Sleep is out of the question. While I was confident that I possessed the three passports to success—a sleeping bag, a packet of oral contraceptives and several addresses—Sydney, I knew, would be no pushover. It would be very racy and very *big*.

I arrived early on a Sunday morning to find it very deserted. The only sign of life was a newspaper whipping down the gutter and a seedy little man in a greatcoat leaning into a corner. Where was the high life, the extravagant bohemianism, the glittering sophistication? My disappointment turned to anxiety when the seedy little man started following me down the street, muttering lewd things and taking sips from a bottle of meths. The miserable dawn had the smell of sea kelp and stale beer in it. Half an hour later I realised that I had taken the wrong direction and was lost somewhere in the semi-slum area of Ultimo. Eventually I took a taxi. I will always remember that drive as a kind of surfacing from the cold ocean depths up into the light. Sydney revealed its beauty coquettishly, lifting its grey, obscuring veils with each passing mile. By the time I reached Bondi I was dazzled by it, converted to it, thoroughly seduced by it.

Previously I had thought of cities simply as places where more people lived and therefore more things happened. Social cesspits. I had never associated physical beauty with them—that belonged exclusively to the country. I stood on the beach, raised my eighteen-year-old arms towards the apartment blocks rising like honeycomb out of the cliffs, and proclaimed Sydney mine, all mine.

1987

37

THE CITY AND THE BUSH

Life on the Low Side

I thought when I returned to Australia from that cold, dank, loveless pit called London—where grey smog dribbled through the skylight, where my poor displaced cockatiels dropped guano disconsolately on the furniture, where the pot-plants needed threats and buckets of chemicals to grow, where nutcases on trains were the only visible sign of *joie de vivre*, where poverty, misery, ideological factions and literary lunches were the order of the day—that I would enjoy living in Kings Cross.

And I did for a while.

I enjoyed rediscovering the pulsating heart of my favourite city. Where I could find a good Italian coffee at 3 a.m. Where there was a poolroom and cheap restaurants. Where I didn't have to walk through sleet to catch the tube, only to discover there was a strike. Where the ancient tradition of dropping by for a cuppa and a chat was not yet dead. Where there was a feeling of renewal each morning after the street cleaners had left.

I found myself a lovely flat with wrap-around windows and lashings of sunlight (the harsh, brittle stuff, not the reluctant, watery kind I had left). And the *space*. My God, two bedrooms. I had lived in a rabbit hutch for the same price in London.

But luxury is always relative. Slowly the seediness of the environment began to percolate through the cracks in my ivory tower, along with a tenacious and reckless breed of cockroaches. I began to feel I had made an error in setting down my first, fragile roots in the Cross.

There were four incidents that led to this change of heart. The first was watching a tattered, battered old alcoholic, mad with the effects of his drug, approach a prostitute, sick with the effects of her drug, on a street corner. He kept pestering her until she kicked him in the shins. He hobbled away in tears. At the bottom of the heap of life there are no sides to take.

Then there were the teenage lads who gathered for booze and boasting beneath my workroom window. I would be forced to listen to them lie about how they'd beaten X to pulp, or taken Y out for a gang bang, or robbed Z of his wallet. They hadn't even grown facial hair yet.

Maybe they weren't lying. Maybe they were the ones who burgled my flat. Twice. I didn't care all that much about the passports, papers and money. But did they have to steal those personal treasures that have an aura of love about them—those irreplaceable mementos of the past which are valueless in the pawnshops? Did they pass their hands over those objects and say: 'Yes, it will hurt her to take this'?

Along with their muddy footprints in the bathtub (they climbed up the drainpipes), they left behind the feeling of violation, of someone unknown, brutally emptying the drawers of their most intimate secrets.

For days afterwards I fantasised about what I would do to them. Would I capture them, tie them up, then lecture them and make them read books until they broke down and promised to change their ways? Or would I Kung Fu them, letting them know that it's not *always* a good idea to pick on the apparently weak?

Mostly, I thought about what would have happened if I'd been home when they called.

I began locking the windows.

The final incident, the one that shook me most, had me sitting bolt upright in bed at 3 a.m., hair prickling up and down the spine, listening to a glass-shattering scream ricochet around the bedroom.

My friend and I raced to the window. There below us was a chap in a spivvy white suit attempting to strangle a woman over the bonnet of a car. Words failed me. Luckily, my friend had dealt with this sort of thing before. With awesome menace he growled , 'Take your hands off her, you bastard, or I'll break

42

every bone in your goddamn body.' My friend would have had to leap twenty feet down to do it, so it was a bit of an empty threat, but the tone of his voice was enough to stop the man and to turn on every light in the next three blocks.

The girl fled; white suit turned in circles, trying to work out where the commandment had come from. He found us dangling out of the window. My cowardly self wanted to duck, but I managed to stay behind my friend, peering over his shoulder.

White suit spoke. 'You shouldn't have done that, man. It's none of your business. She's *my* girlfriend.'

Seized with anger, I wanted to blow his brains out.

When you start thinking like that, it's time to move on.

October 1982

Ghosts Walk the Bush
by Night

How cosy, how pleasant, how healthy, to be writing this under the sickly white light of my primus lamp, outside my tent, having built up the fire to relieve the frostbite in my fingers, defecated in the bushes, brewed myself a gargantuan billy of coffee, and smoked my only cigarette.

Apart from those rustling noises just outside the ring of light, which could be an axe-wielding psychopath sneaking through the bracken (but is more likely to be a wallaby), and apart from the fact that the halfwit puritan within me forbade my bringing cigarettes and whisky, I think I'm going to enjoy this ten days alone in the bush.

It's been a long time since I claimed some solitude in this blessed landscape; since I've done without life's little props. Here I have no friend, no dog, no radio, no clock, no phone, no roof, no body pollutants. The clackety-clack of the typewriter travels out into the valley and gets lost in expanses of forest and paperbark swamp. I'm the only soul around.

This morning, when I woke, the sky was as blue as a morning glory. Fairy wrens, sweet, busy things, handfuls of feathers and bone, flittered through the bushes. I crawled out from my warm, stuffy swag and stirred the embers, which were still hot from a late night under the stars. The dew lay fragile as glass cobwebs; blue woodsmoke chimneyed up through the flowering wattle; the billy sang and bubbled; friar birds quarrelled and gossiped. *Whoosh*—two swept past, slicing the air into a thin arc. The magpies waited for me to leave, like petty thieves.

Although it's a bit lonely stuck out here in the middle of nowhere. All that lyrical Mother Nature stuff, all that myriad-greens-tunnelling-off-into-the-depths-of-the-forest stuff may sound nice, but the point is that now it's night. And that's different. The bush, which was so glorious and welcoming this morning is downright malevolent now. And those eucalypt trunks that disappear into the leafy blackness above don't look at all reassuring. And the various books on rape and murder that I chose to bring with me are not helping my night phobia one bit. What was that noise?

At sunrise I set off down the track that leads up from the darkness, the valley and the mist. By the time I reached the sandy bend of the creek, where it spreads its waters into the swamps, the sun had begun her work. I took off all my clothes and washed in the icy stream. The water curved like smooth brown muscles around the ti-tree trunks. I hid behind the reeds and watched the birds lift and settle on the marshes. I lay on the sand and let the heat dig deep into my city-suffering bones.

By afternoon, the day had changed. It had an eerie feel, as if someone were watching. The sun rolled out from the cool, grey clouds, modulated the key briefly back to the major, then receded again, leaving the bush silent and pensive. The mood absorbed me too—mournful, secretive, inward.

Is it true then, that I carry the collective guilt for all those countless, nameless murders of the people who lived here before me; that I project that guilt and fear on to Nature herself? I felt so today, as if their shadows, having sunk into a deeper darkness, moved among the trees.

The other problem is that it's all very well breezily telling your editor that you'll dash off a couple of columns while you're out bush, but nothing really happens out bush. Try entertaining your readers with a gripping account of how many rabbits you counted Wednesday evening or a 700-word review of a sunset.

But there is ample time to think, as I stare mesmerised into the coals. There's not much else to do really, except flash the torch out into the darkness in the hope of pinning down that accursed noise.

Where was I? What I tend to dwell on out here is: why this universal, constant, enervating war between the selves which neither wins? Purist-perfectionist versus fun-loving health-destroyer; gawping-gullible versus smirking cynic; lover of solitude versus reveller in intimacy; Daughter of Nature versus friend of adrenalin-in-the-gutters-of-big-cities; rationalist by day versus believer-in-ghosts by night. Which to listen to? Which has precedence? Why can't they just take turns, equitably, and leave us some peace? The stars hang like sequins from the lacy, black acacia branches. God, I'd love a cigarette.

September 1982

THE FIRST JOURNEY

The First Journey

My first impression of Alice Springs when I stepped off the train into a cold desert dawn was its architectural ugliness, a complete contrast to the magnificence of the country that surrounded it. But, after two years there, I had fallen in love with the place, and made half a dozen friends without whose help my journey would never have begun.

One of these was Sallay Mahomet, an Australian-born Afghan, whose people had emigrated to Australia with the first imports of camels to open up the central desert area. After listening to my cocky little story, about how I wished to obtain three camels, please, to carry me and my belongings across 1300 miles of desert to the west coast, his response was, 'And I suppose you think you'll make it too.'

His doubts were justified. I knew nothing about deserts, even less about camels, and I had no survival skills whatever. About all I had going for me was a certain pig-headedness, which sometimes protects one better than cynicism, and a need to do something with my life that for me, at least, held meaning.

For two months I worked in a pub, saving pennies and learning Alice Springs from the gutters up. I had no friends, and the people I approached to find out about camels usually laughed in my face or smirked behind my back. It was then I met a European who ran a camel farm on the outskirts of town. We made a deal. I would work for him for a year and in return he would give me three fully trained beasts. I worked seven days a week from before dawn until after the sun went down and two nights a week I worked as a waitress in town. Life was not easy. The only thing that kept me going was the fact that I was learning constantly about these extraordinary animals.

(Camels are intelligent in the extreme, charming, witty, yes witty, hard working and utterly delightful, if a little recalcitrant at times.)

Predictably enough, the deal I made with the camel trainer didn't come through, so I went, at last, to work for Sallay whose attitude had softened somewhat. As he said, if I could stick it so long with the 'maniac', I could probably survive the desert. We made an agreement that if I would help him train some wild camels he had brought in from the bush, he would give me two of the best.

What I learned from the previous fellow were the finer points of camel handling; what I learned from Sallay was the rough and tumble—the fact that these animals could kill. He also taught me how to carve nosepegs, to tie knots, to fix saddles and to do one hundred other little things I would need to know 'out there'. At the end of three months, I took my choice of camels and went home to Basso's farm—a roofless ruin three miles north of town. The camels were both female (bulls are dangerous when they come into season in the winter months). One was an old dowager called Kate; the other a pretty but wild young thing I named Zeleika.

The next few months were bliss. I thoroughly enjoyed my solitude; it was such a relief. Zeleika eventually had a fine black calf—Goliath, who would be a wonderful asset on the trip. I could tether him at night and be fairly certain that his doting mother would not wander too far. But in the midst of my complacency the first disaster struck. Kate, who had sat on a glass bottle, was now seriously ill. I had hired every vet in town to dress the wound, I had even knocked her out with nembutal and had it drained, but now she had reached the point where it was kinder to shoot her. I led her a mile out into the hills and put a bullet through her brain. I had never done such a thing, and it left me feeling empty, sick and shaken.

The 'maniac' had left for parts unknown, and new, inexperienced people had bought his ranch. I offered to work for them in exchange for two camels. It was early winter and the bulls were coming into season. One evening I was teaching the new owner how to hobble the camels when Dookie, a young brown bull, suddenly attacked me. Ten minutes before he had

50

been a little lamb, now he was a raging, frothing daemon. It took half an hour to get him under control. The owner was aghast. He immediately offered me two young bulls, Dookie and Amarillo (Bub), for a small figure. At last, I had my three camels.

One morning I went out as usual to bring them in, and discovered that Bub had a stake right through his foot. It didn't seem possible. I was jinxed. For weeks I nursed him, sticking syringes into that foot, torturing him with injections of antibiotic, changing his bandages and hoping that he would not have to go the way of Kate. When the puncture seemed to be healing a little, I let him roam with the others. And then I lost them, or rather, they lost me. They just disappeared overnight, poof, just like that.

Oddly enough, under my ravings, fury and tears and beneath my thirty-six hours of tracking and searching and hiring of light aircraft etc., I was secretly pleased. It was a perfect 'out' for me, because now I had an excuse for giving up all this madness and going home to Sydney. In my heart of hearts I had never believed I would get this far, and I was afraid. But find them I did (they were shame-faced and apologetic), and now I had to face the fact that this trip of mine was not only possible, it was *going* to happen.

So then the panic set in. I had to weld the saddles and make the pack and stitch the harness and I had to go through the gruesome procedure of castrating the bulls.

I was so broke that I had to go to the *National Geographic* to ask for money in return for my story. I waited until the last possible moment to do this. It was completely contradictory to the spirit of the trip. I did not want a photographer along, I did not want anyone else involved. There seemed, at the time, to be no other choice. If I wanted to continue with this thing, I had to compromise.

And then it was time. Sallay and my father trucked the camels sixty miles west of the Alice, where I would say my last goodbyes to family and friends. They all had that sinking sensation that they would never see me again; I had that sinking certainty that

I would have to send messages from Redbank Gorge the same day saying, 'Please collect. Muffed it first 17 miles.' But we said our goodbyes and, leading the camels, with Diggity my little black dog trotting alongside, I made for the sea, and the last bridge to return to the old self collapsed.

Four days and fifty miles into the journey, my feet were blistered, my muscles cramped. Diggity was footsore and had to ride Dookie—an ignominy she could scarcely bear. Bub was uncertain about the whole venture and Zeleika was a physical wreck. The hole in the side of her nostril in which the nosepeg—used instead of a bit—was implanted had become infected and her discomfort was aggravated by a large tender lump in her udder. Dookie, on the other hand, was having a great time, smiling to himself, looking at everything with smug satisfaction and stepping high. I suspect he always wanted to travel.

We rested for three days in Areyonga, a small Aboriginal settlement in the MacDonnell Ranges. Twenty children watched, appalled, as I inserted a new peg in Zeleika's nostril. I hated causing the camels pain; they thought it was punishment and they had been so good. But I roped her up and twisted her head around and pushed the arrow-like wood through the inflamed wound. Bub, made bold by Zeleika's bellows of agony, snuck up behind me and nipped me on the backside. Camels stick together.

When we had all recovered, we headed off for Tempe Downs Station, forty miles to the south over unused paths through the ranges. I had a compass and relatively reliable maps, but was still uncertain as to my navigational abilities. No one had used the track in ten years and every half hour my stomach would knot and my shoulders tighten as I searched for anything that looked like a path. I got lost only once, but the constant tension was sapping my energy. I realised that this trip was not a game. There is nothing so real as having to think about survival. I was becoming very careful and I was coming right back down to earth where the desert, so welcoming and benign in the beginning, was larger than I could comprehend.

The rituals I performed provided necessary structure. Before I went to bed everything was placed exactly where I wanted it for the morning. Before the trip I had been vague, sloppy and hopelessly forgetful. My friends had made jokes about my forgetting to take the camels one morning. Now it was the opposite—the food was packed away, billy filled with water, teacup, sugar and thermos out, noselines on the tree.

At last I found the well-used station track to Tempe. That night, as arranged, I tried to call Areyonga on my radio set. I had not wanted to take it, but everyone had been so worried I had acquiesced. I still saw it as an encumbrance, an infringement of my privacy and a big smudgy patch on the purity of my gesture. As it turned out, I had a pleasant chat with a fisherman somewhere in Bass Strait, but could not contact Areyonga at all.

Ayers Rock was two weeks away, and I was not particularly looking forward to it. For one thing, I had arranged to meet Rick, the photographer, there, and I was angry with myself for selling out. Secondly, I knew that the Rock was tamed by busload upon busload of tourists. By the time I reached Wallera Ranch, they were beginning to drive me crazy with their cameras and their rudeness. Because of them, I cut across the dunes on a compass course for the Rock. Trudging up and down that solidified sea of sand was exhausting. I decided to ride Bub. And then, 'That can't be real, that blue form ahead of me can't be real.' It floated and mesmerised and shimmered and looked too big. The Rock was too ancient to be corruptible.

Rick arrived the next day. My face was like a viola. He asked me how it had been but I couldn't think of anything to say. I had just led a few camels along day after day, that's all. The truth was that I was beginning to feel this journey belonged to everyone but me. I blamed Rick for this state. Besides, he didn't like the desert, he couldn't see it. He was a New York survivalist and he couldn't light fires, or cook, or fix trucks. He thought the countryside was boring. It was to be some time before I could

53

accept Rick and take the responsibility for including him. For the moment I resented his presence and the interminable photographs he took. Grumbling and sour, I agreed to take him along to the Olgas, and thence to Docker River.

We camped for a week at the Olgas, twenty miles west of the Rock. They are surreal, superb, like a new baking of red loaves set to cool among the sandhills. The camels gorged themselves, Diggity, to my disgust, fell in love with Rick, and I took long walks by myself. But the grandeur of the Olgas obliterated any petty thoughts, and by the time we left there I felt like an Amazon. I had 150 miles of dirt track to follow to Docker River. What could go wrong?

We were only twenty miles from Docker when the weather broke. The weather had been perfect, hot days and cold nights cloudlessly succeeded one another. Now it rained and hailed a deluge. I was carefully leading my camels through a river that had once been a road, when Dookie, the last in line, slipped and landed flat in the water. I raced back to him and tried to get him up. He struggled to his feet and I saw that he could barely use his leg. Out in the bush there is not much you can do with a seriously injured camel except shoot it. And shooting Dookie, my best boy, my wonder camel, was too terrible to contemplate. Slowly, and very painfully, he limped in to Docker River. For four weeks I did not know, and nobody could tell me, whether he would recover. It was not a happy time. Rick had unwittingly taken some photos of Aborigines conducting ceremony and secret business. It set the people against us. When Dookie eventually recovered, I didn't know whether to continue. It all seemed rather pointless.

Robbie D. leaves Docker River with the camels. She is about twenty miles out and she is tired and thirsty. She drinks some beer. She is about to turn off to make camp when through the afternoon light come striding three large strong male camels in full season. Panic and shake, panic and shake. Remember what they told you about wild bulls. They attack and kill. Remember now, one—tie up Bub securely; two—whoosh him down; three—take rifle from scabbard; four—load rifle; five—cock, aim and fire rifle. They are about thirty yards away now and one is spurting a cylindrical arch of blood. He doesn't seem to notice it. They all come forward again. ZZtt this time just behind his head, and he turns and ambles away. ZZttt near the heart, again he's down but just sitting there. ZZttt in the head, dead. The other two trundle off into the scrub. Shake and sweat—shake and sweat.

She unsaddles the camels and hobbles them close, glancing around constantly. The bulls come back. Braver now, she shoots one but he's only wounded. Night comes too quickly. The fire flickers on white sand and the rumbling sound of bulls circles the camp until she goes to sleep.

In the moonlight she wakes up and maybe twenty yards away is a beast standing in full profile. It's beautiful and seems so proud, not interested in her at all. She sleeps again, drifting off to the sound of bells on camels that are peacefully chewing their cud.

Comes dawn and she is already stalking, gun loaded and ready. They're both still there. She has to shoot the wounded one. Another cylinder of blood and he runs away nipping at his wound. She can't follow, she has her own survival to think of. There he is, the last young bull, a beautiful thing, a moonlight camel. She makes a firm decision—this one lives until he does something that jeopardises her safety.

She sneaks around to catch the camels. He watches her. Now last camel to catch—Bub. She can't catch him with that other bull so close. She tries for an hour, she's exhausted, she wants to kill Bubby.

She takes the rifle and she walks to within ten feet of this now excited and burbling young bull. She puts a slug right where she knows it will kill him. It doesn't, and he bites and roars at his wound. She fires again into his head and he sits down, gurgling through his blood. She walks up to his head. They stare at one another. He knows now. She shoots him in the brain, point blank.

Bub allows himself to be caught; she doesn't hit him. Robbie

55

walks on. Sandhills come and sandhills go. Hills rise and hills slip away. Clouds roll in and clouds roll out and always the road. Always the road. So tired, she sleeps in the creek and thinks of nothing but failure. And the next day and the next day, too, the road and the sandhills suck at her thoughts and nothing happens but walking. The country's dry—how can the camels be so thirsty and thin? At night they come into camp and try to knock over water drums. She hasn't enough to spare; she rations them.

She hadn't planned on the sudden dryness. But there'll be water at Mt Fanny, of course. What if there's not? What if the mill's run dry?

At last over the final sandhill. Panic melts and she laughs at herself for being so absurd, an effect of emotional and physical exhaustion, that's all. The threads bind together and she pats Diggity.

The night is dreamless. In the morning, birds—hundreds of them. Of course, where there are birds there's water. Her spirit's high, she packs up quickly, expertly. She walks 300 yards around the corner and there's the mill. The camels drink, Diggity drinks, and she has a freezing early morning bath. Laugh, splash and gurgle, it's good to be alive.

That night she is about to turn in and cars purr in the distance. They stop by the fire and come on over for a look. Aborigines. Warm, friendly, laughing, excited, tired Pitjantjatjara Aborigines returning to Pipalyatjara and Wingelinna. Billies of tea all round. The last car chugga-chugs in. One young driver and three old men. They decide to stay for the night. They share tea and blankets. Early in the morning Robbie boils the billy and starts to pack up. She talks with her companions a little. Two of the old men are quiet and smiling, one she especially likes—a dwarfish man with dancing hands, a straight back and odd shoes on his feet.

I walked off with the camels and who should join me but the little man. He pointed to himself and said, 'Eddie' and I pointed to myself and said, 'Robyn'—which I suppose he thought was 'rabbit' since that is the Pitjantjatjara word for it. It seemed appropriate enough. For the next two days we played charades together trying to communicate and falling into fits of hysteria at each other's antics.

However, after all that had happened, I desperately needed to talk with someone. The community adviser at Pipalyatjara, Glendle, was an old, old friend. I knew his caravan immediately. Who else would have a windchime stuck to a tree in his front yard?

He came out and we hugged and then hugged some more and then we hugged again and I couldn't speak, so I got busy making Eddie and the camels comfortable, and then we three went inside for the inevitable Australian ritual of tea-drinking. I started gibbering then and I didn't stop raving blessed English for a minute.

Eddie was sticking to two things like glue—me and my rifle. His eyesight was terrible so he could not have used the gun but it never left his side. We would walk down to check the camels of an evening and he would carry it on his shoulder and sing to himself.

One of these evenings we passed a group of women coming towards us. One skinny old lady in a faded dress ten sizes too big for her detached herself from the group and wandered over to a few feet in front of us. Eddie squinted and then broke into a delighted grin. They shared a polite and obviously respectful exchange, eyes and mouths smiling at each other.

'Who was that?' I asked.

'That was Winkija, my wife.'

There was such pride and pleasure in his face and such untold respect for that woman in his reply that I was dumbfounded. I had never seen such love shown in a relationship.

The next morning Eddie came to tell me that he had decided to accompany me to Warburton. He needed a few things so we went to the store to purchase them: new shoes and socks and a tarpaulin for Winkija while he was away. He also needed pituri, the Aboriginal equivalent of chewing tobacco, and we walked in total silence looking for the plants in a steep-sided valley. With my whitefella preoccupation with time I worried about getting to Warburton. Eddie did not let time enter his head. Later I learned from him how to relax, not the least of the lessons he was to teach me. He took me through his country and as we went we hunted, laughed, talked and sang all the way. My Pitjantjatjara—the only language he spoke—was almost non-existent, but it's amazing how well one can communicate with a fellow being when there are no words to get in the way.

Neither of us liked cutting back onto the road after our time in the wild country because we had to deal once again with that strange breed of animal, the tourist. It was very hot one afternoon and the flies were in zillions. I had the 3 p.m. grumps, Eddie was humming to himself. A column of red dust hit the horizon and swirled towards us. We swerved into the spinifex, hoping to avoid whoever it was. But tourists have eyes like hawks, and out they piled with their cameras. I was irritated, I just wanted to get to camp and have a cuppa and be left in peace. But they plied me with questions as usual, commented rudely on my appearance (I looked like a Ralph Steadman drawing at that stage), and then they noticed Eddie. One of the men grabbed him by the arm, shoved him into position and said, 'Hey Jacky-Jacky, come and stand alonga camel, boy.' I pushed furiously past this fool, and Eddie and I walked away from them. But they wouldn't let us go. I was boiling, hissing with anger, and reverted to my old trick of covering my face with my hat and shouting, 'No photographs.' But they followed again, whirring and clicking away. Suddenly, all five-foot-two inches of Eddie turned around, strutted back to them, and put on a truly extraordinary show. He turned himself into a parody of a ravingly dangerous idiot boong, brandished his stick in the air, trilled Pitjantjatjara at them, demanded three dollars, cackled insanely and had them all terrified out of their wits. They backed off, handing him what money they had in their pockets, and fled. He walked demurely over to me, and then we cracked up. We slapped each other and held our sides and laughed the helpless, hysterical laughter of children.

The thing that impressed me most was that Eddie should have

been bitter and he was not. He had used the incident for his own entertainment and mine. Whether he also used it for my edification I do not know. But I thought about this old man then, and his people. Thought about how they'd been slaughtered, forced to live on settlements, then poked, prodded, measured and taped, had their sacred objects stolen, had their potency and integrity drained from them at every opportunity, had been reviled and misunderstood and then finally left to rot with their cheap booze and our diseases, and I looked at this marvellous old codger laughing his socks off as if he had never experienced any of it, never had a worry in his life, and I thought, okay old man, if you can, I can too.

Our arrival in Warburton was heralded with the usual cacophony of jubilant children. Rick came, bringing a rifle identical to mine for the old man as instructed. Eventually I called Glendle on the radio and he arrived to collect Eddie. When it was time for Eddie to leave he looked sideways at me for a moment, held my arm, smiled and shook his head. One wave out the window, then he and Glendle were swallowed up in the dust. That month with Mr Eddie was, for me, the heart of the journey.

I had approximately 400 miles to go before I could expect to see another human being. I looked forward to it with a new-found calm confidence. I set off and, after a few hours, decided to cut across country rather than follow the track. There was nothing but sandhills and spinifex and interminable space. I was perhaps treading on country where no one had ever walked before, there was so much room. Throughout the trip I had been gaining an awareness and an understanding of the earth as I learned how to depend upon it. The openness and emptiness which had at first threatened me were now a comfort that allowed my sense of freedom and joyful aimlessness to grow. And my fear had a different quality now. It was direct and useful. It did not incapacitate me or interfere with my competence. It was the natural healthy fear one needs for survival.

At some point I decided that the energy required to traverse sandhills and spinifex outweighed the pleasantness of being away from anything human. I cut back onto the track. The Gunbarrel Highway was two tyre grooves that travelled dead straight as far as the eye could see.

One day I camped in a dustbowl under a few trees. Here would be some feed for the animals and a place where they could roll in the dirt to their hearts'-content. They were unsaddled by mid-afternoon and immediately began to play. I had been watching and laughing at them for a while and suddenly I threw off all my clothes and joined them. We rolled and we kicked and we sent the dust flying over each other. It was the most honest hour of unselfconscious fun I had ever had.

I pulled into camp one night under the protection of two lovely red and yellow mesas, and I sat down to write letters. I kept thinking that I should be wanting to be back where it was safe, and instead I found myself saying that I wouldn't swap places with anyone for anything in the world, that safety was a myth and security a sneaky little devil. To sit by the fire with the billy singing tea shanties and the camels bell-tinkling as they grazed, to wash for the first time in weeks, to spice this drowsy luxury with a momentary rave at a camel investigating the food bags, all this was to me the fullness of life. And straight through my camp came a herd of camels; I did all I could do and then went back to my letters.

I began to laugh. It grew into a great convulsing belly laugh, because, when faced with the truth that when you have done everything humanly possible to protect yourself from death, it was fate, and fate alone, that decided whether you would survive or not.

Again and again along the Gunbarrel I came to that point. It wasn't that I was becoming reckless, it wasn't that I had discarded fear, it was simply that I was learning to accept my fate, whatever it might turn out to be.

All that country was drought-stricken. No vegetation survived at ground level. We struggled into Glenayle station: I must have looked like a madwoman, unwashed, covered in red dust. A lovely middle-aged lady was watering her flower garden. 'How nice to see you, dear,' she said without surprise. 'Won't you come in for a cup of tea?' She pretended not to notice my eccentricities. I found constantly that after a few weeks alone I had forgotten all the social graces.

Eileen Ward and her family were safe enough from thirst on their bore-water; but you cannot water a cattle station with a garden hose. There had been no rain for three years. Nevertheless my camels had a week's hobble-free grazing over a paddock where surviving trees still provided a little fodder high up.

The country I passed through next—the Canning Stock Route— was magnificent, but extremely hard on the camels. They were carrying almost a full load of water and I knew I would have to rest them as soon as I could. From the map, well Number 6 looked promising. I came up over the crest of a high dune to see before me an infinite bowl of pale blue haze with the crescent shapes of dunes floating in it as in a solidified sea. On the horizon fire-coloured sand lapped at the feet of magical violet mountains. I had found the heart of the world.

We skipped down that last dune and made for the creek where I would find the well. I was expecting some puny little wash-away. But, as I rounded the last corner of pine ridge, there below me was a serpentine stretch of green and hard, glittering, white. The camels could see it too, and were straining to get there.

The well itself was difficult to see and overgrown. It was over thirteen feet down and smelled like rotten swamp. But it was wet and would get us by for the necessary few days.

That evening the camels played in the white dust, rising balloons of cloud that the fat red sun caught, burst, and turned to gold. I lay on a foot-thick mattress of fallen leaves which scattered golden jangles of firelight in a thousand directions. Night calls and leaf sighs floated down to me on the breeze and all around was a cathedral of black and silver ghost gums.

The first few days I spent there were like a crystallisation of all that had been good in the trip. It was as close to perfection as I could ever hope to come. I reviewed what I had learned. I had discovered capabilities and strengths that I would not have imagined possible in those distant dream-like days before the trip. I had learned about freedom and security, the need to rattle the foundations of habit. That to be truly free one needs constant and unrelenting vigilance over one's weaknesses—a vigilance that requires a moral energy most of us are incapable of manufacturing. And best of all I had learned to laugh. A profound sense of thankfulness stayed with me through that time. I had extended myself and my view of the world, and that, after all, was what the trip had been designed for. I felt I could sit back now. There were no more lessons the desert could teach me.

Late that night Diggity took a poison dingo bait. She woke me up, sneaking sheepishly back into the swag. 'What's up, Dig? Where've you been, little woofing?' She licked my face profusely, snuffled her way under the covers and snuggled as usual into my belly. I cuddled her. Suddenly she slunk out again and began to vomit. My body went cold. Oh no! No, it can't be, please, not this. She came back to me and licked my face again. 'It's okay, Dig. You're just a little bit sick. Don't worry, little one, you come and snuggle in here and you'll be okay in the morning.'

Within minutes she was out again. This couldn't be happening. She was my little dog and she couldn't be poisoned. I got up to check what she had brought up. My head raced through what you do for strychnine poisoning. You have to swing them around your head to make them get rid of it all. But even if you do so immediately there's hardly a chance of survival.

Diggity started wandering around, retching violently and coming back to me for reassurance. She knew. Suddenly she ran away to some black acacia bushes and turned to face me. She barked and howled at me and I knew she was hallucinating, I knew she was dying. Her two mirror eyes burnt an image into my brain that will not fade. She came over to me and put her head between my legs. I picked her up and swung her round my head. Round and round. She kicked and struggled. I tried to pretend it was a game. I let her down and she went crashing

62

through the undergrowth, barking like a mad dog.

I raced for the gun; I loaded it and went back. She was on her side, convulsing. I blew her brains out. I knelt, frozen, for a long time, then walked back to the swag and got in.

I had never been able to do that before and could never do so again. I shut my brain off and willed it into immediate unconsciousness.

She woke well before dawn. The sick, steely, pre-dawn light was enough to find the things she needed. She caught the camels and gave them some water. She packed her belongings and loaded up and forced herself to drink. She felt nothing. Then it was time to leave that place and she didn't know what to do. She had a desire to bury the dog. She told herself it was ridiculous. It was natural and correct for the body to decay on the ground. But there was an overwhelming need in her to ritualise, to make real what had happened. She walked back to Diggity's body. No, she wouldn't bury her. She would say goodbye to a creature she had loved unconditionally. She said her goodbyes and her thank yous and she went and covered the body with a handful of fallen leaves. She walked out into the morning and felt nothing. She was numb and empty. All she knew was she mustn't stop walking.

I was now about three days' travel from Cunyu Station, the end of the Canning and, as far as I was concerned, the end of the trip. I knew Rick would be there and that Jenny Green and Toly Sawenko might fly out from Alice to see me.

I saw a car coming and expected it to be Cunyu people out to check their bores. Had I known it was the jackals, hyenas, parasites and pariahs of the press I would have hidden. Out they spilled. 'We'll give you a thousand dollars for the story.' 'Sorry, I'm not interested. I just want to be left alone.' 'Oh well, come and have a cold beer, anyway.'

I accepted, as much to find out what was happening back in the world as anything else. They asked a few questions, some I answered perfunctorily. Others I refused to comment on. 'Where's your dog?' 'She's dead, but please don't print that as it would make a few old people back home very unhappy.' 'Okay, we won't.' But they did.

They flew home and made up a story, and the myth of the romantic, mysterious camel lady was created.

That night I camped well off the road in a dense thicket. I decided to wait there for a couple of days. If the press was really after me it would be better to hide out till it all blew over.

I ran into the bushes when the first carload arrived. But I could not still a rising feeling of panic. When they left, I went back to the fire and felt raw. And then I saw Rick's car hurtling past with several other cars chasing him. He came back in five minutes with the cavalcade behind him. He only just had time to give me a vague outline before they all piled out. Some were from the London press, some were from television, some were from the Australian papers. I hissed and snarled at them. I stomped into the bushes and ordered them to put their cameras down.

Rick told me later that I looked like a madwoman—exactly what the press had expected. Yet they shuffled their feet with embarrassment and did as they were told. One man even apologised, after castigating me for not sharing myself with the public.

They left eventually and Rick and I were free to talk. He told me of his own ordeal. Of reading in some overseas paper of how the camel lady was lost, and how he had not slept for four days trying to reach me before the wave of reporters. And it was only then that I realised what I had let myself in for, and only then that I realised how stupid I had been not to have predicted it. I was now public property. I was now a feminist symbol. And I was a crazy, irresponsible adventurer—though not as crazy, of course, as I would have been had I failed.

But worse than all that I was now a mythical being who had done something courageous and outside the possibilities that ordinary people could hope for. And that was the antithesis of what I wanted to share—that anyone could do anything. If I could cross the desert then anyone could do anything. And that was especially true for women who have used cowardice for so long to protect themselves in their male-dominated realities that it has become a habit.

And now a myth was being created where I would appear different, exceptional. Because society wanted it to be so. Because if people started living out their dreams and refusing to accept what is offered to them as normality they would become hard to control.

I arrived in Wiluna feeling like a hunted criminal. But Jenny and Toly forced me to laugh at the insanity of it all. And there were letters from friends and loved ones, plus countless letters from hundreds of anonymous people. Their general message was, 'You have done something I always wanted to do, but never had the courage to try.'

Me, courageous? What an absurd idea.

I spent a week resting and exploring in this ghost town. The spirit of the trip ended for me there. I decided to go on because it seemed appropriate, and because I wanted to take my camels for a swim in the ocean. Rick remained with me for much of that last section. He had shared something miraculous with me that had changed us both and that gave a rock-hard basis to an unlikely friendship.

I had changed my route to avoid Carnarvon. I decided instead to go south to Woodleigh Station where I knew my camels could enjoy a happy and pampered retirement. I loved them all and I knew leaving them would not be easy.

And now I could see the afternoon sun glinting on the Indian Ocean behind the last dune. The camels could smell it, and were so excited they nearly sent me flying. And here I was at the end of my journey, with everything just as fuzzy and unreal as at the beginning. It was easier for me to see myself in Rick's lens, riding down to the beach in that cliched sunset, just as it was easier for me to stand with my friends and wave goodbye to the loopy woman with the camels. I couldn't believe this was the end at all. It had happened too suddenly. There was not so much an anticlimactic quality about the arrival at the ocean as the overwhelming feeling that I had somehow misplaced the penultimate scene.

I spent one delirious week on that beach and, once again, and for the last time, I soared. I had pared my possessions down to almost nothing. I felt free and untrammelled and light and I wanted to stay that way. If I could only hold onto it.

As I look back on the trip now, as I try to sort out fact from fiction, try to remember how I felt at that particular time or during that particular incident, try to relive those memories that have been buried so deep, and distorted so ruthlessly, there is one clear fact that emerges from the quagmire: the trip was easy.

The two important things that I did learn were that you are as powerful and strong as you allow yourself to be, and that the most difficult part of any endeavour is taking the first step. And I knew even then that I would forget them time and time again and would have to go back and repeat those words that had become meaningless and try to remember. I knew even then that, instead of remembering the truth of it, I would lapse into a useless nostalgia. Camel trips, as I suspected all along, and as I was about to have confirmed, do not begin or end, they merely change form.

1978

TRAVELLING LIGHT: AWAY

Rajasthan

I would not have chosen, necessarily, to go to India back in 1979. Unlike most other Australians of my generation and class, it held no fatal attractions for me. I wound up there because I had been presented with a ticket, and Australians are constitutionally unable to look free aeroplane travel in the mouth. Nor was I particularly interested in camels, contrary to what was being said about me in the press. However, the photojournalist with whom I was travelling was to cover a fair in a small village called Pushkar in the Rajasthani desert, where Raica tribespeople brought camels to buy and sell. Thus began a long love affair with that area of India, almost all of it conducted from the other side of the planet.

My abiding affection for Rajasthan hinges upon my affection for some friends I made there. I had returned to Delhi from Pushkar, determined to find out about the Raica. I was given the name of a specialist in tribal cultures, who lived in Jodhpur, but was informed that he was showing around a French journalist that week, and so would be unavailable to talk to me. I flew to Jodhpur nevertheless, hoping that I could at least meet the man.

A dozen people disembarked with me onto the melting tarmac. One of them, a French woman, walked up to a very striking Rajput gentleman. I thought he must be the folklorist, so I screwed up my courage and asked him if he were Khotari-sahib.

'No,' he said, 'but I know Goamal very well. By the way, haven't we met somewhere?'

'Why, no,' I stuttered, looking around at the alien vastness, 'I shouldn't think so.'

'But of course, you are the woman who took the camels across Australia. You must come and stay with me and my family. Yes, I insist,' etc.

I spent my last week in India with Narendra Bhati Singh, his father, Colonel Mohan Singh, and his sister, Minu Sajjan Singh, experiencing a generosity and hospitality that I have not found anywhere else. I had planned to spend six months with Minu in her fort in Ghanerao the following year. But life never goes according to plan. When I did return, last June, Narendra had become minister for tourism and had moved to Jaipur; Minu had come more or less out of purdah, and the Colonel was as charmingly eccentric as ever. The generosity and hospitality remained the same.

This time I was being sponsored by the Indian Tourist Commission, who had arranged accommodation for me in the hotels which had once been maharajah's palaces. Oh, that Rambagh Palace Hotel in Jaipur. Huge, cool room, vast bed, exquisite Indian paintings on the wall, peacocks in the Mughal gardens, a hand-tiled indoor swimming pool, banquet halls, sandalwood soap, and a glass of rosewater brought by friendly staff—decadence at its best.

In the cool of the evening, I sat with my friends in their garden, while peacocks cried from tree-tops, servants brought too many whiskies and a gypsy snake charmer sat quietly on the lawn. We moved inside to have a meal in that most elegant and comfortable of rooms—the paradigm of rooms from which all other, inferior rooms derive. That is, a Rajput sitting room, which consists of a wall-to-wall mattress, covered in coloured cloth, cushions and bolsters; a few beautiful hand-made objects placed on white walls and a slow fan beating from a high ceiling. We were served food on miniature carved tables, and ate it with fingers.

That is what rooms should be: that is how food should be eaten.

Jaipur was founded by the astronomer prince Jai Singh in the sixteenth century. The city nestles in rugged, goat-eaten, pink cray-paz hills—the Aravallis. These are strewn with great plates of shiny stone and covered by a fuzz of acacia. In fact, if you imagine Alice

Springs, subtract Bess-brick ugliness and replace with rose-coloured domes, corbels, carved lattice palaces and mansions, plonk a fort or two on the MacDonnell Ranges with walls along the ridges like dinosaur spines, throw away long socks, bermuda shorts, and navy singlets and replace with turbans and gold earrings or swirls of red, green, blue, yellow silk, shot with silver, add an ancient observatory, a few elephants, and enclose the city in a seven-gated fortified wall, you have, more or less, Jaipur.

For Jodhpur, see above, but leave out the pink and put in a fort-museum of such over-the-top splendour that it makes you dizzy.

Jai Singh's observatory is my favourite haunt in Jaipur. The instruments are masonry sculptures, which measure time, declination of sun, altitudes of heavenly bodies, with extraordinary precision. After climbing over these wonders for an hour, I felt faint with vertigo and heat, so my driver took me to some ruins in the hills above the city. Only monkeys and crows inhabited this wilderness. Below us, pale sand dunes swamped flat-roofed shacks on the outskirts of the town. A murmur from the city rose up to where we sat, rasped by the wind.

Afterwards, in the market, I bought flowers for my friends. No simple flower-seller this. He sat cross-legged under a tarpaulin, behind a mass of blooms. I pointed to roses and tuberoses. It took him ten minutes to create a posy of such sweetness and delicacy—individual blossoms strung on silver thread intricately tied into the bulk of rose petals. Even flowers in India must undergo the rigours of decoration.

I had been in the country only a week. Because of my shyness in asking for boiled water, my stomach had finally given up its battle against invisible bugs. It was time to help it along with some drugs. A warning on the first packet said: 'This drug causes damage to the optic nerve with continued use.' On the second, a warning said: 'This drug causes cancer in rats and mice.' I decided to sacrifice my stomach to my optic nerves.

The dumping of dubious Western chemicals is having a disastrous effect on the villagers. Western medicine, having once been available only to the rich, is now seen by the villagers as a status symbol. People trustingly wolf down large quantities of such pills, and receiving injections is very *in*. Meanwhile, the West discovers homeopathy, and turns it into big business.

From Jodhpur, the last leg of my journey was to begin—an overnight train ride through a dust storm, to the most beautiful place in the world: Jaisalmer.

'It is said that, to travel to Jaisalmer, one needs a body of stone, clothes of iron and a heart of steel.' My perennially smiling guide was leading me through the medieval lanes of the city, where cows and kohl-eyed children jostled for space, brightly coloured silks hung over filigree balconies, camels pulled carts over cobbles, women washed clothes over open drains. We were heading for the Jain temple, containing thousands of statues of Buddha in the lotus position and staring out through glass or enamel eyes. Below the temple, an ancient library was filled with manuscripts written on wood and palm leaves.

Until Bombay became the trade route to Delhi in the nineteenth century, Jaisalmer was the only entry from Central Asia. The whole city is constructed of carved golden sandstone. From miles out in that pale, dusty desert, you can see the walled city on its hill, and it seems impossible that such a thing could exist outside of imagination or dream.

When I first went there, years ago, there were only two places where tourists could stay. Now there are little hotels everywhere, tucked away in ancient alleys. Jaisalmer has been 'discovered', which, as everyone says, somewhat sadly, is a good thing. Tourists bring money and money is what India needs.

My guide continued: 'The towns are built by man, but the villages are made by God.' And that is what I had really come for this time—a camel ride through the villages of the Thar. To do this in mid-summer had a touch of lunacy about it. Even the train journey from Jodhpur had been gruelling. We had come through a sandstorm and by the time I arrived I was smothered in Thar desert grit, which had turned my hair as brittle as spun glass and left small sand dunes in my nose and ears.

But first, my friend Narendra had arranged for a group of folk musicians to play for me, out in the dunes twenty miles from Jaisalmer. The ancient sarengi player arrived first and showed me his press clippings—fragile yellowing bits of magazines clad in plastic. Then came the khamayacha player, the dholak player, the morchung player and, of course, the harmonium player. We piled into Jeeps and sped west.

Fat pink sun bulging into the horizon; silky dunes silvered where the wind fuzzes the edges; musicians singing shamelessly evocative songs; light fading into night, so that the singers, with their white dhotis and bright turbans, become silhouetted against a thickly studded sky; and a lot of alcohol. High romance, this.

Bagaram the guide sat behind me on the saddle, singing and drumming his fingers on my back. The sun had not yet come up. The camel, Babur, was urged into a pace. I was urged into song. It was like riding a cloud, or a piece of satin. It was cool enough for me to throw a sarong over my shoulders. We flew into the desert morning, high as kites.

By the time we stopped at the first village, the heat was ferocious. There were only four huts, almost hidden in the hills. The door of one was covered over with brush, which we removed, then stooped to enter the coolness of a tiny round room, made of stone, and plastered over with dung and mud.

Bagar took off his turban and knelt by the miniature fire pit. He lit a fire with a couple of miserable sticks, then put two cushions against the wall for me. He cleaned out the chai pots with sand and water, then proceeded to cook dahl, and marrow with chilli— our only food, apart from warm beer, Limca and goat's milk, for the next two days. Everything was done methodically, deftly, and with a minimum expenditure of precious resources like wood and water. We chatted for a while (amazing how well one can communicate with half a dozen words and a lot of sign language), then I drifted into a doze. Two crows in black and grey three-piece suits woke me up a few hours later. Bagar was out in

73

the still-blistering heat, chatting at the well with some goat-herders. They sat still as rocks. Nothing moved out there but the dust.

We milked a goat, had another hot chai and set off into the evening.

We visited various Hindu and Moslem villages, dismounting a few hundred yards from the huts. Bagar would explain who I was, and the welcome was always warm, if a little mystified. People would gather in the tiny courtyards, smiling and curious, then we would drink tea and try to talk.

What on earth do these people do, where do they go, in a drought? The desert is eaten out by goats. It seems nothing could survive, even in the good seasons. Yet not only do they survive this border-line existence, they do it with grace, tolerance and charm. And *hut* is hardly the right word for these masterpieces of simplicity and elegance. I turn to my diary now, an almost illegible scrawl written that night in Bagar's home village.

I must remember everything—the bells on the camel as it sits next to me, eating; my string bed and leather pillow; the boy Beru, swaggering to show me his very own camel; Bagar inside cooking, never still, as energetic as a boy; an old man coming to teach me goat-hair spinning; a girl in a tiny whitewashed room, spinning white wool; goats and camels fed and tethered for the evening; pale yellow huts with whitewash around the low doors; stone shelves and various little recesses for storing coloured cloth and a few household goods; on one of them, a rubber thong; women coming in from the wells with clay pots on their heads; an old man chopping at a lump of sandstone to make a lintel for a new house; another showing me how to make shoes; a frail old man singing to his granddaughter; three new-born goats in my room; big brass woks for carrying hay; birds like dyed sparrows kicking up a racket.

74

All night the goats call, and those vile cattle, so confident of their own safety, rattle over stones and lick at God-knows-what. A woman comes at night to talk with Bagar, her whispering drier and softer than the wind, her body a dark drape with bracelets catching at the light. She talks and talks and I wonder what it is about. Universal gossip? Family intrigue? Bagar nods, shakes his head, smiles, as required.

In the morning I was brought sweet chai, handed a bottle of water with which to wash, and directed out into the dunes. By the time we set off, that desolation of stone and sand was already riddled with mirages.

When I returned to Jaisalmer, a day later, I was feverishly planning to return to the villages. I have done a lot of travelling in my time, but I have never, anywhere, enjoyed myself as much as I did in those tiny huts, or been so impressed by how a group of people live.

But no doubt the years will pass and my love affair with Rajasthan will continue unabated, but unconsummated.

November 1985

Across America on a
Harley-Davidson

There is no stretch of highway in the world more boring than Route 75 through Ohio. After hours of staring at soggy flat farmland, from the back of a Harley-Davidson, through billowing truck fumes and drizzle, my first glimpse of the truck stop cafe was a welcome, if surreal, relief. The American mid-west breakfast of two eggs, bacon, sausages, hominy grits, french fries, pancakes, carcinogens and sodium nitrite was to keep us alive until we reached California, where, miraculously, as soon as you crossed the border, you began eating beansprouts, whole-wheat bread and spinach salad with blue cheese dressing.

There were at least 200 trucks parked outside this three-acre extravaganza. Truck drivers who wore ten-gallon hats, T-shirts ('I'd rather push my Harley than ride a rice-burner'), turquoise and silver belt buckles, and snakeskin boots with toes so pointed they could open envelopes, jostled for position at the food counter, or crowded into the space-invader rooms, or riffled through back-copies of *Easyrider* in the reading rooms, or quaffed beer in the bars, or filled their tanks at the forest of gas pumps. Everything a truckie ever wanted or needed was there, including cowboy-booted squaw-tasselled truck-groupies hanging provocatively and vacantly around the doors. Our breakfast neighbour eyed us suspiciously until he found out we were from Australia. 'What's it like livin' in one of them goddamn socialist countries? I hear tell you can't even carry guns there. Man, I couldn't live without mah guns.'

Since leaving New York, three weeks before, we'd been living out a 'Leave it to Beaver' re-run. I don't think I could have tackled it without my genuine, padded, press-studded, black leather Harley-Davidson motorcycle jacket. Not only did I walk taller when I had it on, and feel meaner and look tougher, but the human sea in the streets of Manhattan parted before me. It was, as a leftie journalist had said when the first space shuttle went up, 'biblical, man'.

And after the torment of a three-week publicity tour, I needed any props I could get. When I wasn't collapsing in Hyatt hotel rooms, or being powdered up for chat shows, or fearing for my life on aeroplanes, I was holed up in the cavernous splendour of a white, well-appointed loft in Soho, where chemically fed pot-plants watched my back; where subdued jazz played on the FM; where endless replays of Reagan getting shot (his theatrical *pièce de résistance*), interspersed with doctors' reports and static, played on the TV; where sirens played on the streets; where there were two phones with buttons and dials and red flashing lights, neither of which I knew how to work; where the taps required an IQ of 500 to be turned on; where rows of fumbly security locks on the front door, lift buttons, lift door and apartment door did nothing for my paranoia because any thug could climb up the fire escape and break a window; and where there were only frozen orange juice, Best Foods mayonnaise and fifty rolls of film in the fridge, because everyone ate out. Except me.

So I rang Steve, who joined me from London a week later. When he suggested we buy a motorcycle and ride from New York to California, where he was born and raised, but hadn't seen for ten years, I barely put up a struggle. The thought of wind in my hair, the freedom of the open road, and dying instantly under the wheels of a Mack truck seemed almost appealing. The only things I had against the idea were the possibilities of either spending the rest of my life feeding mashed bananas to a quadriplegic or waking up in some mid-west hospital, unable to remember my own name. There was also in me a deep resistance to being second in command. If Isabelle Eberhardt—that eccentric Victorian wanderer—hit the nail on the head with 'life on the open road is the essence of freedom', she qualified that with 'no one is free who is not alone'. Quite.

And I was ignorant of bikes. I didn't like them. I had no intention of ever learning to ride one. I didn't even understand bikie language. Riding to me has always meant a relationship with an animal—horse, donkey, camel even. You don't ride a machine, you sit on it. Nor was I good 'bikie moll' material. Good bikie molls sit on the back and keep their traps shut. They don't whinge. They aren't back-seat drivers. When the bike breaks down, they don't blame the driver, er, rider. There was a lot I had to learn.

It was raining when we went to pick up the gleaming black and silver sin machine. It sat at the back of the shop like a poisonous insect. While Steve talked with the proprietors about teflon sprockets and eighty-cubic-inch shovelheads, I strolled around the accessories. Was this an S and M outfitters or what? I picked out the most expensive helmet (I like my brains where they are) and then my gaze alighted on the leather jackets. I took one out, tried it on and, hey presto, transmogrification. I placed my fag between my lips, squinted through the smoke, put my thumbs in my pockets and ambled back to the guys. They spoke to me! I now understood how the invisible man felt when he put his bandages on. 'Great deeds and great thoughts,' as Camus said, 'all have a ridiculous beginning.'

Ah, the intoxication of speed as we hurtled from beneath the broken teeth of Manhattan's skyline and onto the freeway. After the first thirty miles, I started loosening up. Enjoying it even. There was, after all, some pleasure in not being the one in control. My limpet-like clutchings, the involuntary shutting of the eyes when we leaned into a corner, were being replaced by stunts: the standing up on the pegs to give fist salutes to other bikers, the leaning back on the sissy bar to roll a smoke, and the moving from cheek to cheek to relieve the growing numbness in my bottom. After a hundred miles the discomfort was intense, the grumbling loud. Harley-Davidsons are not designed for the comfort of the bit-of-rag on the back, they are designed for the comfort of the rider, and for style. I was hunched on a stylish vibrating fence-post and feeling resentful.

I tapped Stevie on the shoulder (he was singing 'I just wanna ride on my motorcyyyyy-cle'. Could this regressed maniac be the man who had seen me through thick and thin in London?) and asked him to stop at the next sports shop. We were bound for Vermont, and there were no sports shops. There were drug stores, which sold invalid's inflatable toilet seats. I had no shame; I bought one. I was willing to risk my credibility with the bike fraternity, but my buttocks, never. I grew very attached to that cushion over the next three months. If Flann O'Brien was right about molecular transference, then Steve was becoming more like a bike, and I was turning into . . .

We rode ten hours that day, across the Adirondacks, around the swooping bends of Lake Champlain, through the first sweet hints of spring—polluted only by those totems to the American Dream: the omnipresent cars and billboards, the gas stations, the baseball caps and the fast-food franchises. America is a car culture, constantly travelling to greener pastures. Americans do not see the horror, junk and pain littering the way. There is always a new frontier to head for, so how much you bugger up the one you're on is irrelevant. This faith in the future at the expense of the present comes from moving fast with the windows wound up.

By the time we arrived at our friends' country house just outside Hinesburg, we were exhausted. We couldn't talk. We drooled. They put us to bed. I was too tired to attack Steve for bringing me on this torturous and pointless journey. But after three days with them, during which we gum-booted our way through Vermont's mud season (apparently not its finest) and stuffed ourselves with home-made apple pies, and swapped vitriolic reminiscences of book tours and reviewers, the desire to be off hunting for new frontiers began to infect me too. The first burst of acceleration as you leave somewhere in the early morning is almost worth the increasing tedium of the following miles.

Our plan was to head for Canada, turn south, then follow the setting sun. But when the first flakes of jet-stream snow bit into my face, I knew it was a rotten idea. We put all our clothes on, till we looked like marshmallows, and wrapped scarves around our faces, but still we could travel no more than twenty miles without having to stop for coffee to thaw out. We decided to go due west to Ohio.

Now, all this time I had been pestering Steve about camping out. Motels were expensive and, anyway, I wanted to sleep next to the earth and watch the constellations and build warming fires and sing songs and communicate a little with Mother Nature, whom I hadn't seen in quite a while. 'I think you'll find camping out in this country a little disappointing after what you've been used to,' was all Steve had said. I couldn't imagine what he'd meant. Camping out is camping out. It's driving off the road into the bush and looking for wood and boiling tea and giving in to pantheism. How could that be different anywhere?

After gasping and gagging through Detroit air, I insisted that we stop at a camping spot the map showed us on the shores of one of the Great Lakes, thirty miles outside that blighted city. It was getting dark, but still Mother Nature was nowhere in sight. Just more black slums and a nuclear power plant. Yes, our camping spot was a patch of mown grass, nestled beneath this glittering structure, and just off the freeway. There was no wood. There were no trees. Just rows of trucks and vans parked on the grass. The entrance fee was eight dollars. This barren patch of horror was second home to whites who could no longer find work in the city and were now employed by the plant. They saw their families on weekends. They were worried.

We rolled out our sleeping bag a little way from the edge of the lake. Decaying rubber thongs, used condoms and dead fish littered its putrescent shores. Vile garbage smells wafted into our puckered nostrils; repetitive clangings of nuclear reactor machinery sang us to sleep. We had entered the throbbing heart of the American nightmare.

By the time we reached Kentucky, the graffiti in the ladies' toilets had changed. No longer the simple sexual references, or the diagrammatic genitalia. Even the 'I love Bud' scribblings and the arrowed hearts gave way to purely religious references and fire and brimstone sentiments as the southern accents grew thicker. However, the blue grass country was indeed beautiful, the weather was warm, and my spirits were thawing. We stopped in at a diner for a BLT sandwich and a beer.

That tiny backwoods diner was the antithesis of the dreaded Ohio truck stop. It had the best jukebox I've ever come across: 'Howlin'' Wolf, Bo Diddley, Mance Lipscombe, and some of the most obscure and brilliant country and western I've heard. When we told the waitress that we were taking the Harley to California, and thence to Australia, she looked wistful, then puzzled and uncertain. 'Well, ain't that somethin'. I always had the ah-dea there was some water twixt us and them.' By the time we reached Tennessee the graffiti was not only biblical but racist as well.

Everyone has been told horror stories about the south. Steve said that during the sixties he'd been run out of towns he'd had no intention of stopping in. But we not only had no trouble, we were treated with utmost courtesy. Even the Harley, an erstwhile symbol of the evils of northern degeneracy, got some appreciative comments.

Things had certainly changed. The south suffered such a whipping during the civil rights movement, so much bad press had taken the heat off the north, which was equally guilty of repression, and which was still ripping it off economically, that the southerners were now bending over backwards to prove, especially to foreigners, that they were just regular friendly folks. And if that friendliness never got beyond the 'have a nice day' level, if that friendliness was only a millimetre thick, beneath which lay the stuff fanatics and Queenslanders are made of, we were never around long enough to worry about it. We spoke to very few blacks. They cast their eyes downwards, smiled apologetically and crossed the street before any contact could be made. Not here the cocky confidence of New York blacks.

One night, on the banks of the gurgling Mississippi, our appreciation of the southern mystique deepened. The campground was a gravel pit and, because the freeway was only a few yards away, we had difficulty sleeping. Eventually we unplugged our ears and listened to our neighbours—a plucky little Nashville crooner and his sad, monosyllabic wife. Spotlighted by the bulb that dangled outside the cement toilet block, they were singing Hank Williams born-again songs to the tinny accompaniment of a plug-in guitar, and passing the baseball cap around to the lumber-jack-shirted occupants of three Ford pick-ups, all of which had bibles and rifles in the back.

We learnt when to interject with 'praise the Lords' and 'hallelujas' while a pretty fourteen-year-old girl, all painted up for her big night out, sat among the rifles, bibles and men, and did not move, speak or breathe as they cracked smutty sexual and nigger jokes and slurped Cokes and sang gospel songs. Even such inroads to an understanding of what lurks beneath southern hospitality could not tempt me into dallying. Truth and Consequence, New Mexico, was still a long way off, and anything might happen.

Something did: my first Oklahoma tornado.

I'd been sitting on my cushion, watching rainclouds gather, wondering if I was going to get wet as well as bored, and mulling over the difficulty of coming to grips with the meaning of life on the back of a bullet travelling through ever-changing visual stimulae.

It's not that there isn't ample time to think—it's that it's usually on the level of what you are going to eat for lunch. Persig or no Persig, here was no inward journey. When you ride a machine, you are always on your way to somewhere, you are never actually 'there'. When you walk, you are always 'there' and can never get away from 'there'. It gives you time to ponder and be changed.

On a machine you are protected from change. That, after all, is potentially revolutionary, and there is little room left for that in America, where whole communities set off in roving bands of mobile homes with appropriate names like 'The Invader', taking not only their colour televisions and kitchen sinks with them, but also their neighbours. For all America's reverence of individualism, it is of the strictly manipulable kind.

I was jolted from this reverie by a claw-like black cloud scudding across the plains. My, but that cloud is travelling fast, I thought. Suddenly there were swarms of clouds, boiling clouds, furious clouds. We were on a freeway—the next exit was a few miles on. Stevie revved the bike until we were zooming through the most electrifying spectacle I had ever witnessed. Until, that is, I spied the funnel.

For all those who have not turned off an American freeway on to a dirt road at 120 miles per hour, don't try it. Unless, of course, you are being chased by a black, lightning-fringed finger of death. We escaped it—just—and spent the next few hours in a tiny village called Pink, sheltering from the hail and violent winds. Nothing like a bit of adrenalin to bring you back to reality. We stayed a couple of days with an oil-drilling friend in Norman, but I was anxious to get to the deserts, where I was sure a gnawing sense of displacement would be cured.

There are many good reasons for visiting the States, but, to my mind, the two that stand out like Manhattan's twin towers are tasting, for the first time in your life—in a down-at-heel roadside restaurant on the outskirts of a ghost town whose name you will never remember—real Mexican food and real Margaritas, and seeing, also for the first time in your life, the astonishing wonderland of the south-western deserts. Put them together, add a bike and good weather, a soupçon of snow-capped mountains in the distance, and you've a recipe for hedonistic joy.

Perhaps it was the sudden injection of chilli rellenos, tequila and vitamins, perhaps it was the high altitude, piney-woods country of Arizona, perhaps it was the sniff of the arid zone that made my spirits soar but, whatever it was, by the time we flew through those vistas of limitless forest, rolling green into grey into blue, I was feeling on top of the world. By now I had replaced my helmet with a scarf—had become a convert, in fact, to the anti-helmet-law lobby (because, let's face it, if you do bounce off your bike at eighty miles per hour, no feat of engineering ever designed is going to keep your grey matter from spilling). You feel better with it off, you see more, you don't suffer from neck strain, you can hear birdcalls distorted by Doppler effect, and if you're going to be mad enough to ride a bike in the first place, you may as well go the whole hog.

Enough has been written about the marvels of the Grand Canyon, and all of it under-statement. The place is magnificent. But the tourists and the prices began to grate, so we headed for Monument Valley—John Ford country; home of what's left of the Navajo. It was, if anything, even more awesome than the canyon, and to which no film or photograph could do justice. Mile after mile the endless flatness stretched on, interrupted only by towering monoliths of bare rock and the occasional eagle wheeling through the wall of silvery heat shimmer, rising up into blue-black sky. This was what I'd been looking for. This was where the heart was.

While Australian deserts have a more unearthly, prehistoric, mythological quality, while they demand more depth of feeling, the American deserts take the cake for sheer brazen grandiosity and impact. They don't grow on you, they hit you in the back of the head like a mallet. Away from the reservation itself, where we were required to stay on the roads, I was able, for the first time, to sleep in the sand dunes, and to walk out into the desert as far as I could and not see a fence, or a path, or a soul.

Coming from Australia, I had considered this privilege a right. But in America nature was fenced in—under glass. For most people the pleasure of being alone in the wilderness was a thing of the past. The bush had become an alien, dangerous and distant thing. Control is the name of the game, and I wonder how Australia will deal with the same problem, which it eventually must, as all the wild places are taken over by multinationals and tourism. Our extraordinary freedom to move where we like will become the privilege of a select few. This recurring theme, of seeing Australia's future in America's present, was what disturbed me most. That Australia is learning nothing from American mistakes, that we are swallowing all the worst aspects of the dross and spillage of the American Dream.

We strolled along the well-graded National Park paths, and read plaques informing us in large print that some European explorer had discovered the place, and then in small print at the bottom that an unnamed Indian guide had taken him there.

Some things are the same the world over.

Two days later we were surrounded by the chintz and tinsel of Las Vegas. (If you can possibly wean yourself off the silly notion of including Las Vegas in your tour of the south-west, do so.) We drove down the main street and headed right on out of town. Death Valley was far more appealing.

The temperature on the road now was up to 130 degrees. We put wet clothes under our jackets and wrapped wet turbans around our heads. Driving for hours in such heat, even with interruptions for swims in tepid canyons, or for tinkering with a sick and overheated Harley, or for praying for your life as the bike lunges from side to side in the turbulent winds of mountain passes, has a debilitating effect on mind and body. It begins to bend you a little. It rakes at your flesh like claws. It passes out of the realms of mere scorching into some uncharted territory of pain. Camping out that night didn't appeal; I wanted crispy sheets and air-conditioning.

We pulled into a motel on the shores of Lake Mead—a tin-pot joint with a bar and gaming room across the street which, like all bars in Nevada, contained perpetual night for the benefit of gamblers. We soaked for hours in hot water (high velocity grime takes weeks to shift), then turned the telly on to the local news. An atomic bomb had been tested 150 miles north that day. 'What????' I was anxious enough about contracting cancer in this region, what with all the uranium tailings left on Indian reservations for the kids to play in, and what with actors dropping like flies because they'd been on location in this country, without having to contend with fallout.

After a sleepless night, during which I imagined I was being penetrated by deadly and invisible beams, we packed up at dawn. The cleaning lady arrived. I grabbed her arm and, with alarm in my voice, asked her if she'd heard the dreadful news. She smiled indulgently at this poor stupid foreigner and, with a certain pride, said, 'Goodness, honey, there's nothin' to worry about. They go off all the time. Sometimes they're so big the walls shake. I think it affects the pot-plants a little, you know, but we're used to it around here . . . and it's better than being overrun by them I-ranians.'

'Steve, get me *out* of here.'

Death Valley. Second lowest point in the world. Weird moonscape mounds of borax, distorted by the heat mirage. (The temperature had climbed to 150.) Gold had been its original attraction, and the fever and madness that commodity has always inspired in the hearts of men led them to die in that desert in multitudes. Hence the name. There is *nothing* alive there.

The heat after 9 a.m. was impossible. The heat after 6 a.m. was impossible. We made a pact that we would travel on in the cooler hours, so when we called in at Furnace Springs— a truly glorious oasis with a pool and bar and groves of palms— we had several hours to fill in. Now, I had made certain rules at the beginning of this trip. One was never to travel over seventy miles per hour if it could possibly be avoided, another was never to drive after dark because Steve had next-to-no night vision, and the other was no booze. A cold beer here and there, okay, but no hard stuff. Steve found this one difficult, because his favourite hobby—after riding bikes—was getting drunk.

He had done well so far. But one drink led to another, and, while I swam in hot spring water, Stevie swam in cold beer. He didn't get drunk, mind you, just a wee bit unreliable. By the time we were ready to leave, the gas station had closed. We had to siphon petrol from a car. Stevie siphoned, and he siphoned and he siphoned. There was a small hole in the hose. He looked ill. He nearly passed out. He got rid of the nasty taste with yet more beer. 'Steve, don't you think we'd better . . .' 'I'm fine, Rob, jus' fine,' he said, through a cheesy, cross-eyed grin. He chuckled and danced a perfectly straight line just to prove it.

It was dusk and down to 110 degrees. I didn't particularly want to get on the bike with him, but I didn't want to stay in Furnace Springs either. The first few miles were okay, then I noticed the white line doing curious twists under our wheels. Tap, tap, 'Steve . . .' Tap, tap. 'STEVE.' 'Huh?' 'Stop the fucking bike.' 'What for?' as we narrowly missed the gravel at the side of the road. I began throttling him from the rear. A moon was rising over the nothingness. A scream was rising in my throat.

We camped that night beside the road, the hot wind moaning over us, the grit and borax sticking to our sweating bodies. It was nearly the Waterloo of a perfectly fine relationship. He wasn't even conscious of the kicks and oaths I planted on his snoring form. However, it is impossible to maintain such a level of passion during a Death Valley dawn, especially when you can see ice-tipped granite mountains about to pierce a sinking desert moon, as you travel up into California.

The first indication that we had crossed the border, besides the spinach salads with blue cheese dressing, was a west-coast denizen decked out in flapping multi-coloured paraphernalia passing us at a hundred miles an hour on his bike, with his feet up on the handlebars (I don't know how he managed it either), Walkman earphones clamped over his flying tresses, and a beer in his hand. Stevie's spirits were rising. He was recognising his roots.

California has deserts, mountains, lakes, San Francisco, oceans, Redwoods and oysters. Unfortunately it also has Californians. We spent a month there during which time Steve, in his search for the past, looked up many old acquaintances—who, he discovered, were either dead from heroin overdose and violence, or had changed from rabid pig-hating People's Park supporters to avid Ayn Rand aficionados. I think it almost broke him. Had we not stayed with his oldest friend Eric, I think he would have bitten more than one ghost from the past on the leg. But I shall come to Steve's tequila sunrise in due course.

There was now a certain urgency in our travels, which even California's lakes and mountain passes did little to pacify. By the time we reached Sacramento, tradesmen's entrance to the west coast, Stevie was like a bloodhound, hot on the trail of home. Back in New York he had casually let drop that because we rode a Harley we might end up fraternising with members of various bike groups along the way, and that I shouldn't worry, he would handle it. It wasn't that I had anything *against* the Hell's Angels or the Gypsy Jokers, but the thought of smiling wanly at forty toothless, tattooed, oil-soaked fourteen-stone brothers in the middle of nowhere and maybe blowing it was not my idea of fun. I had walked out of *Mad Max*. I knew about those guys. So when we called in at Sacramento to buy a new chain, and when the shopkeeper didn't have the tools for putting it on the bike, and when a toothless tattooed oil-soaked fourteen-stone brother kindly invited us back to his place so we could use his gear, and when Steve said okay despite my daggered looks which stuck six inches out his back, I died. I died.

We spent the afternoon at a little suburban house—Steve in the garage with twenty or so members of the Sacramento chapter, tinkering and talking about bikes, and me in the kitchen with our new friend's wife, talking about her kids, her husband and bikes. They completely dismantled my preconceptions about the Hell's Angels, but I'm glad we weren't black and riding a rice-burner.

On the crest of a windy hill that evening, we stopped to look at a finger of fog stretching across the Golden Gate Bridge into the bay, and rolling banks of it about to snuff out the lights of that lovely city: San Francisco—our destination. In Nevada we had bought the kinds of fireworks that were illegal in California, so we were warmly welcomed by Eric, a charming ex-pyromaniac who featured big in Steve's tall tales of sixties' insanity, who used to build cannons for a hobby and was now a jeweller, and who had mellowed a little with age and travel. Until we arrived. I noticed Eric's eyes glaze over and memory stir as he fingered the bottle rockets. The city was kept awake until the wee hours by overgrown, giggling five-year-olds and deafening explosions.

Despite such promising beginnings, despite hearing some of the greatest musicians in the world playing in small, intimate bars, despite making forays to the Santa Cruz Mystery Spot or watching seals frolic amongst the seaweed and rocks, the next two weeks brought about a perceptible decline in Steve's spirits.

Going home is traumatic enough after ten years, but when many of your old friends start quoting Reaganisms at you and saying 'let 'em get a job' or 'liberalism is dead', it's hard to remain cheerful, let alone diplomatic. It came to a head when we all headed north to a friend's place on the coast.

Eric forewarned Steve he would find the man changed, so, when we sat down to dinner in his fabulous restaurant that night, and when the chap suddenly, pugnaciously and without warning leant across the table, pointed his bobbing fork at Steve and said, 'I suppose you think I've sold out, just because I worked my butt off for this restaurant? Well, I'm sick of feeling guilty and it's about time we Americans grew up and forgot all that crap about Vietnam and the welfare state—I mean, let 'em get a job. America has been the whipping boy for too long, and now it's time for good ol' American know-how to take us back to the top,' Steve merely said, 'Let's not argue; I think your restaurant's wonderful and good luck to you. The food's great.'

'No, come on, man, I can see it in your eyes. As Ayn Rand says . . .' The conversation was downhill from thereon.

Back at his mansion it continued to plummet, as his wife chimed in with how the women's movement had been and gone in America, how it had worked, and was now just a lot of screwed-up dykes causing trouble. We all drank too much, which never helps. I eventually went to bed, unable to bear the strain of smiling through clenched teeth. Stevie had that dangerously belligerent light in his eyes so, when he came in to say goodnight and told me that if his friend didn't stop looking for an argument he'd have to worry him round the ankles like a bulldog, I knew there'd be trouble.

Eric carried him into the bedroom at seven in the morning—an incident with a crossbow, a run-in with a woodpile, and three bottles of tequila later. I lay next to his unconscious form as long as I decently could, but eventually had to get up and socialise with the offended couple. I had to, with the help of the wonderful Eric, smooth the troubled waters until three in the afternoon, when a sickly, cross-eyed, tequila-sodden wreck staggered out of the bedroom, farted, said thanks for the lovely evening, and left on his Harley with me on the back saying yes, lovely, do hope we see you again, do hope your ankles heal soon and sorry about the crossbow, ha ha. We nursed our hangovers in the giant Redwoods.

A week later I took a Harley and a shell-shocked friend back to Australia. Whatever lingering doubts he had had about wanting to live in his home-country were cured forever. As for me, the only permanent injuries I sustained from the journey are a small, numb patch on my bottom and a cemented trepidation about current American thinking.

I wanted to end this piece saying something positive, appreciative and lyrical about Australia's Big Brother, wanted to convince myself that all the wonderful people we met there and all my expatriate Yank buddies and all the good thought that comes out of there make up for the born-again nuke 'em mentality that pervades the place. But for the life of me I couldn't do it. Except, of course, that it's a hell of a nice place to visit.

December 1981

TRAVELLING LIGHT: HOME

Useless Loop and Hopeless Reach

One should never go back. Just as the castles of one's childhood turn out, in later years, to look like workers' cottages, so the emotional charge of the sacred sites of one's personal history dissipate over time until they look and feel just like anywhere else.

I had been hankering to get to Shark Bay, where I ended my camel trip all those eons ago. Not that Perth wasn't pleasant, Fremantle even more so, and the south-west corner as delightful as all those tree-lovers had cracked it up to be. But, ah, I could hear the desert singing to me, tugging at unseen strings in my sternum.

One hundred years ago, Marcus Clarke described it thus: 'The dweller in the wilderness acknowledges the subtle charm of this fantastic land of monstrosities. He becomes familiar with the beauty of loneliness ... he learns the language of the barren and uncouth, and can read the hieroglyphs of haggard gum trees ... distorted with fierce hot winds ... The phantasmagoria of that wild dreamland termed the Bush interprets itself, and the Poet of our desolation begins to comprehend why free Esau loved his heritage of desert sand better than all the bountiful richness of Egypt.'

The beauty of loneliness was not to be mine this time, because I was travelling with a friend whose notion of travel rather differed from mine. For him it meant taking a cab between air-conditioned hotels. He had not come across the idea that a bed could be portable and rolled out under the stars. But I had described my dream landscape to him so often, and with such mad fire in my eyes, that he, too, was infected by the spirit of pilgrimage. His enthusiasm was somewhat dampened, or rather evaporated, by Denham, as my diary records . . .

'Ah,' we sighed, Friend and I, as we placed empty diet lagers on the westernmost table of the westernmost pub at the westernmost end of the universe—Denham, to be precise. Well, no, Monkey Mia is the *precise* end of the universe, Denham is its gateway—if you step through the gate you drown in the febrile blueness of the Indian Ocean.

We managed a wan smile at each other. We had driven here through midday mirage, sitting on the melting upholstery of our four-wheel drive. I ordered more beer, and then I saw them. A strangled cry escaped me, and I turned pale under the purple of skin that is unaccustomed to temperatures greater than sixty Celsius. Yes, synchronicity had delivered Mr and Mrs Cruelty and Despair to us, yet again.

This couple had dogged us all the way from Perth. We had been obliged to listen while these two attempted to murder each other with words. They made any references to the beauties of nature seem laughable, e.g. Mr and Mrs C and D thrust knives into each other's underbellies and twisted them in order to maximise pain, while a bulging sun sank into the febrile blueness of the Indian Ocean.

But I must avert my face from these two, researcher into the human soul though I am, and describe instead my wonderful holiday in WA, where I thought rednecks were in retreat until I left the thin strip of coastal belt, where jukeboxes, once wonderful-weepy with Slim Dusty, Charlie Pride, Hank Williams sing-alongs, are now international-homogenous and where prohibitive signs have proliferated like fruit-flies over the past eight years.

We skolled our beers, re-entered the wall of heat outside (anything was better than the bickering couple) and strolled to the end of town. There, waiting for us, was yet another prohibitive sign. It was all too much for Friend. 'Signs,' he screamed. 'Don't spit here, do not deface this sign, do not defecate within ten yards of this sign. I'm sick of signs. I'm going to take *direct action*. I'm going to *liberate* this sign.' With that, he ripped up the sign saying 'do not liberate this sign', and threw it into the ocean.

He had reached an understanding of the concept of 'going troppo'.

The first part of our drive north had been wonderful, despite the mind-bending heat and the threat of running into the Cruelty and Despairs. By the time we hit the four-wheel drive tracks from Lancelin to the Pinnacles, I felt I had come home. This was it. This was what I remembered—the wildest, most beautiful part of the planet.

The Pinnacles are part of the Nambung National Park, which is described in the tourist blurbs as Western Australia's best-kept secret. They go on to say that the roads are going to be upgraded, so it need be a secret no more. Alas, how true.

We drove into the shifting dunes in a luminous glassy pink light. The sky was like rose quartz. The dunes were fuzzed silver at the edges by the wind. Is there anything in the world more glorious than desert at twilight?

'Um, where's the road?' Friend was hunched over the wheel, peering into the pink. 'Oh, sort of over there,' I ventured. It was no good, the light was fading and so was the road, fading and fraying into sand-covered nothingness.

It took us all of the following day to drive the fifty miles to the Pinnacles, so impossible was the track, and so often did we stop to frolic at bore tanks, or tumble down white sand ridges. The thought of even seeing another footprint had drifted into the impossible. We were deliciously lost, oblivious to the heat, kicking gypsum dust between our toes, free at last of the constraints of civilisation, and then . . .

A sign saying 'Keep Left'.

I let out a howl of fury. There was nothing but flies and a couple of fishermen's huts for miles; what did they mean, those goddamn gingery, over-muscled park rangers with their beards and zoology degrees and nothing to do all day but make up visual pollution in the form of rustic signs. We kept right, until the Pinnacles.

These twisted, freakish shapes are, in fact, the calcified stumps of tuart trees, God knows how old. There are thousands of them, pricking up out of yellow or red sand dunes. We wandered for hours, and then, greenies forgive me, I did a terrible thing. I *camped*. Yes. I walked a long way past the dunes, rolled out my swag and boiled a billy.

It's not that I don't, in my cooler moments (back in the city), agree entirely with the National Parks mentality. The pressure of countless tourists in four-wheel drives necessitates rigid control. But what about those of us who want to get away from all that? Where can we go now that everything is either behind private fences, or inside National Park boundaries, now that the bush has been Americanised and made safe?

The country has to be protected from locals too, as we found to our dismay. We had called in to a station homestead and the owners had cheerfully told us how a National Park had refused to let them graze their sheep so they had got a few mates together and set fire to it. Friend's eyes crossed at this point, but I kicked him under the table and he kept his trap shut.

Having had my fix of stars, billy tea, and sand in the swag, we pushed on to Kalbarri. Progress had passed through here as well, transforming a small fishing town into a tourist extravaganza. However, I knew a stroll through the Murchison Gorge would revitalise my wilting spirits. Unfortunately, it didn't get the chance, because halfway down the slope I succumbed to heat exhaustion and Friend had to cart me back to the caravan.

Never mind, there was still Nilemah to go, and after that dolphins, and stromatolites and Useless Loop and Hopeless Reach . . . but I am getting ahead of myself.

Nilemah. When I lived in London in a urinal laughingly referred to as a flat; when I was driven almost to suicide by the spectre of a line of slimy, grey, brainless English pigeons, with missing legs, cooing for food at my window each morning like crippled beggars, what kept me smiling? Nilemah, that's what.

I daydreamed that this little house made of shells, situated on a primordial stretch of coastline thirty miles from the nearest neighbour, a stone's throw from the stromatolytes (a species of primitive coral which is 500 million years old and exists almost nowhere else on earth), I daydreamed that one day it would belong to me and my camels. So when we drove in, even the sign that said, 'Keep out, beware nailboard traps, trespassers prosecuted', did nothing to dint my optimism.

Did my chin tremble when I saw it? Perhaps. Friend reached out and patted my shoulder. We sat in silence and contemplated a roofless ruin full of sheep shit, woolly carcases, crows, broken bottles and graffiti. One must never go back.

The following morning we went for a dawn stroll down the beach, paddled among the algal mats, and watched emus bathing in a glowing lavender ocean. Then the owner of the station found our camp in the bushes and told us to piss off.

All this brought with it a perceptible decline in my spirits. Caravans began to look good to me, all those clean Laminex surfaces. So we sweltered for a day in one at Monkey Mia, where tame dolphins came in to the beach to charm the tourists and turn them into drooling idiots. I admit it, I drooled. There is something about stroking a free dolphin while it looks up at you with those human eyes that is indescribably moving.

After Denham and the incident with the sign, I decided to give Useless Loop and Hopeless Reach a miss. The thought of driving through heat shimmer over impassable roads for a day only to find hordes of marlin fishermen zooming around in, or the Cruelty and Despairs bleeding all over what I consider to be the most spectacular land-sea-scape in the country (where six-foot rollers from Madagascar crash into barren cliffs and sing through blowholes, where you can see turtles making love in the sea, where there are reefs and parrot fish and salt-bush and shifting dunes)—that thought was more than my heart could bear.

So we drove straight on to the camels, which were waiting for me, or rather, waiting for the dozen packets of jelly beans I had brought. As we drove west, the temperature rose approximately one degree every six miles.

We spent a couple of days on the sheep station, feeding jelly beans to the beasts, or sitting in the swimming pool with our hats and sunglasses on, while willy-willies blew red grit and scorpions into the water, and spinebills and mistletoe birds dropped dead out of the trees.

Then, hey ho, the camels were persuaded to climb aboard a truck and be taken, protesting, to a new home in the south. By the time Friend and I had dealt with all that, and got ourselves back to Perth, we were filthy, camel-bespattered, baked, exhausted shadows of our former selves.

We booked into the Sheraton (eyebrows were raised and noses were held) and when we reached the sanctuary of our germ-free, deodorised, insulated, air-conditioned, luxury-appointed, blowfly-free room and fell upon a non-portable acre of bed, I had to admit that as much as I loved my 'heritage of sand', it was nice to indulge myself with the 'bountiful richness of Egypt' occasionally.

May 1985

Ayers Rock

In the 'dead heart' of Australia, about two hundred miles south-west of Alice Springs, stands the most symbolically charged object in the country. Even city-dwellers, who have never visited it, will regard it as a quintessentially Australian monument. Europeans have been in this continent only two hundred years and anything that enhances a sense of national identity is clung to with desperate sentimentality.

The Pitjantjatjara Aborigines, to whom the object is profoundly significant, have been here for at least fifty thousand years. They believe their 'country'—a vast tract of desert spreading into three States—forms an axis about which the universe turns. Ethnocentricity perhaps, but when you gaze for the first time at Ayers Rock, floating like Leviathan in a sea of orange sand, it's easy to agree with them. It's like nothing else on earth.

It rises, isolated and improbable, over a thousand feet above the dunes. From a distance it is difficult to appreciate its size but, as you travel closer, its grandeur begins to penetrate your consciousness until, walking around the four-mile base, you are receiving a powerful dose of what Borges called 'the wonder distilled from elementary things'.

Ask geologists how it was formed, and they will tell you that unimaginable pressures transformed mud into stone dense enough to resist the processes of time which ground the surrounding land into grit. The Pitjantjatjara hold a different view.

In the beginning, before the world took on its present form, carpet-snake people journeyed from the east and settled at a sandhill containing Uluru waterhole. Meanwhile a party of venomous snake-men were creating havoc among all the other ancestral people. They came from the west and camped twenty miles from Uluru, where Katatjuta (a mass of mountainous pebbles), now exists. From there they set out across the plain to attack the harmless carpet-snake people.

What followed was a bloodbath to rival the Trojan wars. At the close of the creation period, or Dreamtime, Ayers Rock/Uluru rose up—a monolith bearing all the physical and metaphysical signs of that epic battle. A waterhole in the side of the Rock is the blood of a dying carpet-snake man; a fragment of stone— the severed nose of a venomous snake warrior; a large cave— the mouth of a woman weeping with grief for the loss of her son, and spitting 'arukwita'—the spirit of disease and death— over her enemies. Some of these sites are so sacred that only fully initiated Aborigines may go there.

Ayers Rock is particularly rich in Dreaming stories, being an intersection of many different mythic odysseys. Wallaby people, spirit dingo, and willy-wagtail woman all contributed to its topography. As every contemporary Pitjantjatjara is a direct descendant of one or another of the totemic heros he or she is an integral part of the landscape created by that progenitor. Ancestor, descendant, 'country', storyline and ritual art form an eternal continuum.

To traditional Aborigines then, the Western concept of owning country is not so much ludicrous as obscene. This mutual incomprehension regarding the *meaning* of land still forms the basis of cultural conflict. When Uluru National Park was 'handed back' to the Pitjantjatjara under the Land Rights Act, that conflict found an emotional focus.

I first visited the park over a decade ago. I had been walking for two weeks without seeing a soul. Up one sandhill, down another, and on either side of me an infinity of dunes stretching away into blue. I was not looking forward to the Rock, having overdosed on its shape on billboards advertising life insurance, on postcards promoting the wonders of the Centre and on T-shirts sold in kitsch shops in Alice Springs. But when I saw Uluru shimmering on the horizon, I was spellbound. It was too ancient to be corruptible.

I spent a week there, exploring every cave, fold and gully of it. There were three small motels at its base, a little shop, and some houses for the rangers. Aborigines lived in their humpies just outside the settlement; tourists wandered into those camps taking photographs and being generally insensitive. I spent a further week at Katatjuta before continuing west into blissful emptiness.

A few years later the Pitjantjatjara were granted freehold title to the park, which they then leased back to the government. They had a say in its management, and they received a share of the financial benefits of tourism. The hand-over ceremony was, apparently, very moving. White Australia had made a gesture towards acknowledging its genocidal past.

Three months ago a friend arrived in Alice Springs for a holiday. I had planned to take her to some of the lesser-known beauty-spots—not yet visually polluted by rustic signs, garbage bins and tourist buses—but the greenhouse effect wrecked my itinerary. Dry riverbeds had turned into torrents and all the roads were cut. At least we could fly to the Rock. It would be covered in waterfalls—a rare enough sight to make it appealing.

'I hope you don't mind roughing it,' I said, remembering the dilapidated caravan I had stayed in last time. (Several years ago Yulara village was built twenty miles north of Ayers Rock, to house the tourists and take the ecological pressure off the Rock and the social pressure off the Aborigines who still lived at its base. I imagined a conglomerate of prefab buildings and porta-loos—hardly romantic, but adequate.)

A decade is a long time to live without experiencing the sandhill country of Central Australia. When I got off the plane I decided to give in to nostalgia and pantheism and walk the five miles to Yulara. My friend climbed into the bus, along with all the American, Japanese and German tourists wearing funny hats.

Oh, the unearthly beauty of the dunes. They were the colour of conch shells, of rosebuds. Thanks to the rain, there were explosions of colour everywhere—purple parakeelya, bright yellow grevillea, blue shrubs sprouting scarlet flowers, silky orange trunks of desert poplars, and, furring the ridges of the dunes,

101

pincushions of pale green spinifex. I struggled to the top of a sandhill and there it was, bruise-coloured, striped by waterfalls, and capped with grey mist. The rain came down in buckets but what did it matter? I was strolling through an infinite garden, I was there and I was happy ... Until I turned a corner and saw Yulara. This was no village, this was a *town*. An architect-designed town with Sheraton hotels, a mock Greek amphitheatre and tourist-trap boutiques. 'My God,' said my friend, when I found her huddled in the motel-style room complete with television and microwave, 'this place is a space bubble. If you step outside the force-field you fall into the void.'

When the shock had worn off we covered ourselves in green plastic garbage bags and scuttled across to the tourist information office. The vision that greeted us was straight out of Baudrillard— a large group of people absorbed in watching a video of the very landscape they could see perfectly well through the wrap-around windows. We hired a car and drove straight to the Rock.

As it swelled in front of us the 'oos' and 'aas' from the passenger seat turned into awed whispers and then silence. The 'skin' of the Rock was changing from steel grey to purple to shiny red. We drove right round it, past all the new carparks and rustic signs, one of which invited us to the sunset viewing point—a sandhill from which tourists are instructed to point their cameras at the Rock. Why this particular sandhill in an ocean of sandhills? No one knows. But the tourists obediently line up along it by the hundred, snapping away. It is a remarkable and dispiriting sight.

Having completed our circumnavigation, we parked the car, took off our shoes, tied on our plastic bags, and stepped out into the freezing wind. The path took us around the western face, past the white line painted up the side of the Rock. A sign informed us that the 'climbing line' was closed due to slippery conditions. Tourists were ignoring the warning by the dozen and oblivious to the little iron plaques commemorating the deaths of several climbers who had turned into pancackes on the sand below. By the time I had walked a mile I was so numb with cold that I took off all my clothes and plunged into one of the new waterholes beneath a thundering cascade that came down at us from the gods. The water was pure as crystal and so deep in places it was blueish black. We struggled through the needles of rain until we came to another sign notifying the public that this small fenced-off area was a sacred site and must not be visited. A group of tourists was reading it, one of them then crossed the fence and headed off for the cave. I called him back and explained in my most polite voice that the Rock belonged, morally and legally, to Aboriginal people and that he was their guest and that he was about to break their law and as he could explore every part of the rock except two or three tiny sections why did he feel the need to trespass. He told me to fuck off.

We spent the remaining two days in the space bubble, eating and reading books.

Tourism is not the benign industry governments would have us believe. Unless it is rigorously controlled, it can fundamentally alter the natural environment and adversely affect the host culture tourists wish to experience. In the Northern Territory the people most affected by tourism are the Aborigines, yet they are the least likely to receive its financial benefits.

The custodians of Ayers Rock are lucky in many respects. They have the power to veto the use of Uluru. (Recently they turned away a musician who offered enormous amounts of money to make a video on top of it—a new definition of 'rock clip'.) Even so, many of them are abandoning it for more private settlements out in the desert. They don't mind people visiting their country, but do not like being on display or being opted into a tourist industry in order to please a government that is still antagonistic to Aboriginal control of land. They worry about and feel responsible for the climbers who fall to their deaths, and they are powerless against the trespassers who blunder about in fertility caves ignorant of the deep distress this causes.

It may eventually come about that the very element which

attracts so many visitors to Uluru—Aboriginal culture—is swamped by a kind of tourist imperialism.

Which isn't to say that one should not visit this 'wonder of the world', only that history is full of uncomfortable ironies.

June 1989

follow a group of women going hunting. Nothing else seems to be moving. We park the truck beside one of the half-dozen tin houses—basic constructions of one or two rooms, with large shade areas where most of the living is done. A few adults and children are sitting on the ground in the shade. Near them a billy can straddles a small fire and above them hangs a haunch of kangaroo hosting a nimbus of flies.

For the Aborigines living here, Aneltyeye is home in the deepest possible sense. Here they are free of the social distortions imposed by white-run settlements and they are close to bush foods and medicines. But, most importantly, they are near the sacred places that form part of their identity, and that give them spiritual sustenance and psychological strength.

Gloria is there and in the distance I can see old Emily's unmistakable shape—very bent and very small. I am always delighted to see that irascible old woman. She has a quality that transcends cultural differences: 'chutzpah'. She insists we take her to look for pituri. As we drive along almost invisible tracks, we pass an outcropping of rock. Emily begins to sing. Just a few chanted lines under her breath. She is singing to the Dreaming of that place.

Later, everyone gathers at the Arlwekere (specially designated areas where women of all ages meet to talk politics, carry out ceremonial duties, organise hunting trips, look after children and paint their silks). Not for the first time I wish I had my friend's facility for languages. While she and the women mumble on in that indecipherable tongue, the only word that makes sense to me is 'batik'.

Two days and five outstations later. I have dozed off in the Arlwekere, having spent several hours watching the women at work.

First they build low bough shelters, slight protection from sun and wind. Then the fires are made and the wax melted in old hubcaps. The hot wax is applied with brushes and tjantings to cloth supported on mulga branches. Later it is boiled in larger flour drums. Often several women will work together on the larger pieces, sitting together on the orange earth, surrounded by dogs, children and the omnipresent dust and flies, while around them fluid sheets of pure colour flap in the wind beneath a cobalt sky.

A dog scratching by my head wakes me up. Jenny is reading out quotes from the catalogue for the umpteenth time and the women are nodding their heads in approval.

And then it's done. When we get up to leave, an old man invites us to see one of his wooden sculptures. He is proud of it and rightly so. Two snakes entwined around a stump—the essence of snake. It is a lovely thing, out here in its context, but in Alice Springs it will be just another piece of tourist art, stripped of meaning.

There are no jobs available in these communities, and the production of artworks is necessary for survival. But how are the artists to make sense of a value system so different from their own. On the one hand, some paintings, particularly the acrylics on canvas, are attracting international admiration and huge sums of money. The buyers want the paintings to be as 'traditional' as possible. On the other hand, there is pressure on Aborigines to make their work accessible to tourists—kitsch art, simplified and standardised for easy understanding. The attempt to make commercially viable products without violating the rules of traditional systems, or forsaking their own aesthetics is a confusing task. Besides, how can one expression of the Dreaming be worth more than another?

Anxiously the old man asks what we think he will get for it in the Alice. He was worked for days, finding the right tree, chopping it down, adzing it, painting it. 'One hundred dollars perhaps,' we say, wishing we could make it higher. He looks disappointed, but resigned.

Encouraged by our enthusiasm, an old lady comes and asks, in broken English, whether we will look at her painting. She holds up a symbolic Dreaming story, made of tiny dots of acrylic. She wants to know how much we think it is worth, but the language she uses is revealing. She does not say, 'How much will I get for my painting?' or 'How much will I be paid for my work?' she points to the canvas and says, 'How much for my culture? For my country?'

We are a long way from the Pompidou Centre.

February 1989

ALICE SPRINGS

Alice Springs

You travel across a thousand miles of emptiness to get there. You imagine hitching rails, fata morghanas and willy-willies. In your mind's eye you see a roly-poly or two puffing dust down a wide sleepy street. You think of romance, Nevil Shute and gritty, burnt-out faces—skin like ochre and walnut; eyes blue distillations of sky trapped in perpetual squints. Leaning in doorways are homely women, their arms folded across wrinkled but generous bosoms, and under the shade of eucalypts sit Aborigines, exuding the inscrutable wisdom of ages.

You are seeing a never-never Alice through the vaselined lens of mythic nostalgia.

What you find, on arrival, is a desert of red-brick shopping malls, breeze-block suburban dumps proliferating at plague pace, luminous force-fed lawns balding at the corners, bewildered German, Japanese, American tourists forking out guilt money to Aborigines in bandages cadging for a drink. But if you lift your eyes away from the streets and shopfronts, there are the folds of the MacDonnell Ranges floating in the heat haze like slumbering sphinxes. They are unutterably beautiful; they make a joke of the trash at their feet; they have all the time in the world to await, dreamily, their day of revenge.

All the Alice Springs that ever were lie jumbled together, occupying, more or less, the same patch of earth. With every return you discover a new one—more complicated, bizarre and foreign to you than the last. Sometimes you catch a glimpse of the place you remember, fixed as a prop from the theatre of your past, and sometimes the signs of an even more remote town which only exists in the faded sepia memories of the 'characters' down at the Old Timers' home. Or, further still—and here the imagination must be made to leap— a place created by three caterpillars and a beetle at the beginning of time.

I was in Manhattan, packing up to come to Australia. Just as I was about to leave the apartment a phone call came through from my friend J. in Alice Springs.

'The house next door is for sale, are you interested?'

Through the windows I could see morning sun polishing the spire of the Chrysler building and hear the roar of a city driven by human will. If home is where the heart is, then this phantasmagorical island had a large fragment of mine.

'Alice Springs?' I smiled into the phone. I would be going there for a holiday. That's all.

I arrived at 10 a.m., inspected the house at noon and bought it in the afternoon.

'But why?' said an anxious New York voice on the end of the line.

When I first came here, in 1974, Alice was the ugliest little town in Australia. Now it's the ugliest in the world. The town fathers have a kind of genius for kitsch, and, in their greed for the tourist dollar, they have managed to destroy what little charm the place once had. And yet people whose lives have been touched by it feel compelled to return to it, again and again. It's as if we've all been 'sung'.

I remember meeting my first Aborigine. I had been in the Alice about an hour and no doubt wore the stunned expression of the New Chum. Like most white Australians, I had never spoken to, walked past, *seen* an Aborigine. I had read about their culture in books; they were as remote from me as the ancient Greeks. An old black man stopped me in the street. He wore a stockman's hat beneath which was a wide smile. He smelt of camp fires and warm earth.

'Hey, sister, you got a smoke?'

Enthusiastically I handed him my tobacco, thereby demonstrating that not all whitefellas were racist swine. Everything I possessed in the world was with me. Six dollars, a meagre little suitcase, a dog, and that one, last, packet of Drum.

'Why, thank you, sister,' he said, pocketing it, together with the papers and matches. He tipped his hat and walked on. This did not strike me as the behaviour of an enfeebled victim but rather of a born survivor.

I did not know it at the time, but I was a writer, chasing after tales to tell as if with a butterfly net. Here are some of the facts I caught about that long-ago Alice:

A week before my arrival an Aboriginal man was found, painted white, in a gutter. A week after my arrival, a traveller was found dead in the caravan park where I spent my first night, with a branch of mulga shoved into his anus. The town dog poisoner was still at large: he threw strychnine baits into front yards in the dead of night. Aborigines in the fringe camps (small, traditionally orientated living areas on the outskirts of town) lived in abandoned cars, upturned rainwater tanks or under shelters of hessian and plastic. Often they had no water. Some of the pubs still had 'dog windows'—outlets for blacks, usually at the back of the building. A local politician's wife made the public suggestion that Aborigines make themselves useful by pulling rickshaws full of tourists from the airport to the town—a distance of ten miles. Dodgy-looking Americans with reflector sunglasses arrived by Starlifter to work at Pine Gap—the largest US spy base outside America; dodgy-looking South Africans with reflector sunglasses arrived and joined the police force. Territorians consumed more booze per capita than anyone else in the world, and, in the whole of the town, you could not buy one fresh vegetable.

But history, in the form of the Land Rights Act, was about to catch up with Alice Springs and give it an almighty kick in that place where it hurts most—race relations.

I had come to prepare for a journey but, quite by chance, I arrived with the first wave of 'southern do-gooders'—mostly white, mostly young, mostly middle-class urbanites armed with university degrees and idealism—they enlisted in the Aboriginal battle for land and better social conditions.

If much of the heat had died out of political debate in the larger cities by 1974, in Alice it was still blazing. Because here, more than any place in Australia, it was demonstrably true that the 'Lucky Country' was a profoundly racist one. Here, the brutish aspects of the national identity could not be camouflaged.

The Central Land Council—a little grass-roots organisation housed in a dingy building—administered the act under which untenanted desert could be claimed by traditional clans, provided they could prove before a white tribunal that their 'ownership' was authentic. The immense complexity of Aboriginal affiliations to land meant that equally immense quantities of anthropological and linguistic research had to be presented at the hearings which were held out bush in the parsimonious shade of gum trees. Often Aboriginal witnesses had to divulge secret/sacred information if they wanted their land back. I will remember, forever, seeing an old lady, a bundle of delicate bones, obliged to perform a particular ceremonial dance before the judge—everything about her betraying an intolerable anguish.

Meanwhile the anti-land rights lobby, right-wing politicians, anxious pastoralists, avaricious mining company executives, organised themselves. Millions of dollars were spent on scare-tactics advertising; membership of the Ku Klux Klan swelled alarmingly; 'Rights for Whites' graffiti graced the breeze-block walls of Alice Springs. With the headiness of every Aboriginal victory came the demoralisation of many defeats.

In this atmosphere the do-gooders worked absurdly hard for little money. There was no time for doubt and no room for any kind of ideological factionalism. Lunchtime at Sorrentino's (vanished now), would see revolutionary and revisionist, Marxist and Christian, artist and ideologue, young thing and old hand, excitedly, amiably, tolerantly telling jokes, swapping stories and always, always, debating politics. The original group was not large—twenty perhaps. But from all over the world people blew into town—adventurers, bums, academics, musicians, eccentrics and thinkers. It was out on the network that, in Alice, something remarkable was happening.

Perhaps the phenomenon of return (and we do return, all of us, for weeks, or months, or years), has as much to do with nostalgia for an era as for a place. Alice in the early seventies was a hard act to follow. Where else in the world could one be part of such an intensely bonded community, or develop skills in all areas of life from flying aeroplanes to fixing trucks; from learning Aboriginal languages to making radio programmes? Where else could one spend time travelling through awesome landscape, mixing with and learning from a culture as different from one's own as it is possible to be, then return to town where there may well be visiting world-famous authors, film-makers, intellectuals begging for one's opinion over the barbecue. But, most importantly, where else could one believe that one's work was not only necessary, but morally elevated?

Local organisations were formed around specific issues—health, housing, communications. Council for this, cooperative for so and so. They were controlled by Aborigines, but specialised skills were still needed, skills that very few Aborigines possessed. The planned obsolescence of whitefellas never occurred.

What were urban Aborigines, who had suffered the brunt of dispossession, who had lost not only many of their traditions but their languages as well, to make of this? How were they to feel when they visited the Centre, searching for their cultural roots, to find wall-to-wall whitefellas speaking Pitjantjatjara and Warlpiri enjoying long-term friendships with traditional Aborigines out bush and lodged in secure and interesting jobs. In the face of such privilege it was sometimes hard to be generous.

'Nigger farming', as some of the more cynical called it, had become a growth industry.

And now the present. Another Alice Springs, entirely contemporary . . .

I am standing in the main street under something that looks like a giant flying wimple—vast wings of canvas stretched between steel poles. It symbolises the ancestral Yeperenye moth emerging from its chrysalis. The red-brick road under my feet covers its

117

Dreaming track. Whoever designed these banalities found the concept of the Dreaming somewhat difficult to translate into physical form.

One could say that the Dreaming is a spiritual realm which saturates the visible world with meaning; that it is the foundation, or matrix, of being; that it was the time of creation; that it is a parallel universe which may be contacted via the ritual performance of song, dance and painting; that it is a series of stories of mythological heroes—the forerunners and creators of contemporary man.

During the creation period, these ancestral beings made journeys and performed deeds as a result of which there arose the topography of the earth and all that exists upon it. They behaved like men and women, but they were a synthesis of human and thing—plant, animal, element. At the end of that epoch, exhausted by their work, they sank back into the ground at sacred sites, where their power remains in a condensed form.

Not only did the spirit beings give the world a shape, they imbued it with a moral structure—handing down eternal ceremonial and social laws whereby all contemporary humans have equal intrinsic value, and a share of goods. Because no distinction is made between material and spiritual, ancestor, story, sacred site, song and singer are all, in essence, the same thing. Dreaming tracks (or stories, or songs) lace the whole of the continent. Australia, then, *is* a narrative.

It's as if the creative potential of a whole culture, instead of being dissipated on the production of material wealth, has concentrated itself on the never-ending translation of all social phenomena into one elegant, all-encompassing symbol.

In short, the Dreaming is an astounding intellectual feat to which the flying wimple bears little relation.

I step out of its shade and set off down Todd Street. All that is left of the little town I once knew is the skeleton. In this other fleshy place I can buy not only vegetables, but cappuccinos and prosciutto, croissants and freshly squeezed orange juice. I can find French champagne, Italian shoes, Greek feta and Indian

118

spices. To the east is a large casino just near the Sheraton Hotel; to the west, the Diarama illustrates Dreaming stories with the aid of things that look like Barbie dolls. (Morning Star has a coiffed blonde wig.) Where once I would have seen Aborigines, I now see members of that unmistakable tribe—tourists. I pass dozens of shops run by Europeans selling Aboriginal artwork ranging from kitsch to quality. At eye-level there is a congestion of photographs and advertisements semiotically suggesting that, here, contact with 'natural man' may be bought. (A visitor can, for a certain sum, spend a morning out bush hunting and gathering with bona-fide blackfellas, though he might bump into those same blackfellas later the same day buying soft-drinks or booze at a supermarket.)

Yes, the Dreaming has become big business, but at least it's not only whitefellas who are cashing in. The little, struggling, shoestring Aboriginal organisations are now complex bureaucracies housed in architect-designed buildings. Cooperative art galleries sell dot-dot paintings for several grand. The Aboriginal owned Yeperenye arcade houses fast food joints, dress shops and delis.

I head towards Heavitree Gap, then turn east along the ranges until I reach one of the fringe camps—a respectable place now, with houses and sewerage, ablution blocks and garbage service. I am paying a visit to one of the traditional owners of Alice Springs.

Harold Wheelchair Alice is an old man with a long white beard. He sits on a bed on his porch, his wheelchair beside him. A hot, sandpaper wind blows down on us from the hills.

'This my grandfather's and great-grandfather's country,' he says. 'This place was made looooong time ago, when the Yeperenye caterpillar was travelling. From all over the place they come through to here. Utnerrengatye, the woolly ones, they come from east, but our mob, Ntyarlke and Yeperenye, they the green ones with pretty painting on their back. [These bright green and yellow grubs can be found by the million decimating the gardens of Alice Springs. I always think of their invasion as a kind of payback.] You seen that big one there at the Catholic church?'

'The big caterpillar?'

'Yeah, that painting Wenten Rubuntja made; that's a caterpillar.'

(Ancestor, landscape and abstract painting are the same.) 'Oh, of course. So what happened then? How did the caterpillars make all the places?'

'You know where that high school is? Well, that first caterpillar rose up from there. [As Wheelchair begins to tell the story, his whole expression alters, eyes and hands following the direction of his ancestor's journey. I do not know what he sees when he looks at the landscape, but I do know that the Dreamings are as present to him as I am.] He was coming down, coming down the Todd River. He camp one place again, at Ntyarlkerle tyaneme, then he move across to Emily Gap. Then that Yeperenye mob coming down, down, to camp where that mission shop is now. From there they go Mpwetyerre, where that casino is. They camp one night then they come this way through Heavitree Gap. They go to Irrparlpe, where that children's home is, and from there they go right down to where the Irlperenye sleeping.'

'Irlperenye's the green beetle?'

'That's right. Well, he got cheeky, that Irlperenye, and got jealous for all them Yeperenye and he start killing half of them, biting their heads off. So they went to Amoonguna sandhill where that winery is now, but that beetle still chasing them, killing half of them again. So they went round like that to Amoonguna and they leave that beetle halfway. They finish up at North Emily and that's there they are now.'

'What happened to Irlperenye?'

'He stay there at his place. That camel farm on top of him now. [Pause] You seen that dingo there?'

'What dingo?'

'That one in town there. Big rock. They got a chain around him.'

'Oh yes.'

120

'Well that old dog was camping there in the Dreamtime. And mob of little ones, little puppy dogs there too, and that old mother dog. Well that big dog he go to Adelaide and the puppies too, and mother dog and that father dog.'

'What do you mean they went to Adelaide?'

'White man took 'em long time ago. What's his name . . .? Strehlow.' (Strehlow was a famous anthropologist. There has been a great deal of debate and bad feeling over the fate of his collection of sacred objects.)

'Why did he take the dogs?'

'Because they was making that bitumen road to Darwin and puppy dog right in the way when they survey the road. Had to shift them because if they break those rocks, then all the dogs now get cheeky. [There is a story that, years ago, old men used to rub these rocks in the hope that whitefellas' dogs would turn against their owners.] Another old dog, Mount Gillen, he come from South, from Simpson Desert. He brought bush potato from sandhill country. That potato called Mount Blatherskite now. That dog, he come around here and seen that old woman sleeping with her puppies. But that other old man he gallop across from his place and kill him where that salt spring is near the train line. That old dog got sick then, went back and died at his place up north. You go there, you seen a rock in a tree. Aborigine must be put that stone there in olden times. Had to ship it there because railway line coming through here. Took tywerrenge and all [sacred objects associated with the law of specific Dreamings]. Strehlow helped them. Some still down there in Adelaide, in a museum.'

'Do you think they should come back here?'

'Some old fella mob and young ones say we gotta get them back again and put them in cave and all that. But who going to look after them? Early days Aborigines go round all the caves here and look after them properly. No drink those days. But if they bring them back and leave them all over, all the young fellas don't go round any more, nothing, so the white ants will eat them.'

'If they stay in Adelaide, will they be all right? Will they hold their power?'

'Oh yes, they keep their power and they all got their mark on them still. When proper museum here, *then* they come back.'

'You remember Strehlow?'

'I know Ted, the younger one, not that old fellow. He speak all kind of languages, you know. Arrernte, Luritja, Warlpiri.'

'How many do you speak?'

'I speak ... Western Arrernte, Central Arrernte, Eastern Arrernte. And I speak Anmatyerre, Kaytetye, Alyawarre, Warlpiri, Luritja ... oh, and a little bit Pitjantjatjara. Why you laughing? [We are both laughing.] Lot of Pitjipitji people used to get rations here. You know that old stone building other side of the Gap? That was old police station. Mr Sturt was boss there, he had lots of troops—Aborigine troops, too.'

'Aborigines from other places?'

'Yeah, but from here, too. Any Aborigine mob kill a bullock, those troops go and shoot them the whole lot. Aborigine shoot Aborigine, and all. But that early days, eh? Different now. Whitefella used to go out with camel and horses, all over the place, walk around, get prisoners, bring them here and then walk them to Oodnadatta.' (A few hundred miles.)

'Walk them?'

'Walk them! Only the police on the wagon, the prisoners all walking in neckchains. Then they'd put them on the train and send them to Port Augusta. They do their time there, then they bring them back to Oodnadatta and just leave them there. But the Afghans pick them up and bring them back on the camel trains. Afghan mob have fifty, sixty camel. Bring wheat from south, all sort of things. Afghan mob used to play cards with Aborigine mob. Euchre. Funny game. They put two bob or one shilling up. My old people mob used to work twelve month for fifteen pound on the cattle station. Buy lot of tucker, blanket, calico with that from Afghan mob. Then that train-line come and Afghan mob went home. Give all their camel to old

Aborigines. But some stayed. Old Misky, he had a shop. Used to pray a whole lot. All us kids we go there and wait for him to put the mat out, then we'd steal his lollies. He'd be down the creek, three, four hours praying, give us a chance to get all the lolly.' He mimics the old fellow praying, with comic genius. When the laughter dies down, I ask him, 'Tell me more about the caterpillars. There are more stories, aren't there?'

'Oh, big mobs more. Lots of beautiful paintings too. You been to Emily Gap? Seen that big rock painting there? Well, that caterpillar too. Emily Gap a very sacred place. Not allowed to go there early days. Nobody allowed to walk through Heavitree either except Aborigine boss and his warriors. They very rough men. They walk around and see if there's some strange bloke, then they spear him, kill him.'

'What happens today, when the sacred places are disturbed?'

'They used to do that before Sacred Site Authority turnout stop them. Aborigine was just . . . wasn't owner then, government the only owner then, do what he like. Now we tell them not to build on sacred site. They might damage him and make all Aborigine mob sick. That high school is on sacred site. And that Verdi Club.'

'Did that make people sick?'

'Oh yeah. But we got our own turnout now and they got to come and ask we lot where they can build. Early days, all the Aborigine just living in old bungalow. Then they going to make the town white, so they shift us seven miles to Amoonguna. Warlpiri and Luritja and Arrernte . . .'

'Did everyone get on together then?'

'Oh yes, we was good friends those days. Then government said, "You people got citizen right now." [Full citizenship was granted to Aborigines in 1964.] All Aborigines they leave that place then. We were sad because we been friends for long time. Nobody used to fight those days. All good mates, dancing, ceremony, because no "ngkwarle", no grog. Then boss for natives affairs come round and telling everyone, you're allowed in the pubs now. Well every pub then full up with Aborigine. I reckon the drink spoil everything. Everyone went mad and the kids was starving.'

There is a long pause which I don't interrupt. At last he says, 'I used to live at Charles Creek. One day they say, you got to roll your swags early tomorrow and move. "Why?" we say. "Because Japanese going to bomb this place." All the military boss was there, General bloke. They say, "Get ready now." "All right," we say, "we'll get our things ready." Shepherd mob start off that night, taking nanny goats and donkeys way over east, eighty mile. Camels too. Took them at night. Then one hundred army trucks pick up all mission Aborigines. The Japanese make a mess of Darwin, but we were lucky.'

'Where did you go?'

'Arltunga. Native mission there. Some of our people came back from New Guinea, Timor. Real sick. Whitefella too. Skinny. That Japanese mob not feed 'em, eh? I was young man then, went to school there with the nun mob. Old bishop came to us at Arltunga and say, "Oh, all you mob, we got new place for you now." So we got shipped *again*. All the nanny goat, donkey, horses, camel and dogs and we had to take them long long way across the Simpson Desert. Like Moses mob we went travelling. That must have been the Promised Land I think, that new place— Santa Teresa. See we were not many children those days, some die from measles, chicken pox, bad cold, all die. But then we get to Santa Teresa and it was a happy place there. You go there now you see big big mob of people. They grew and grew there. That must be thing like Moses, eh? [Pause] From Arltunga, long time ago, they took big mob of half-caste kids away. From our families they took them. Whole lot of people unhappy. Never see those kids any more.' The old man rubs his hands down his face. 'But at Santa Teresa we were happy.'

'Are you getting tired? We've been talking a long time.'

'Yeah, little bit tired.' He laughs. 'But good story, eh?'

'Yes. A great story.'

I am visiting another friend at a different town camp. When she

124

was fourteen she was as beautiful as the day. She is in her early twenties now and has the ravaged look of the terminal alcoholic. Her face is mashed, her top lip a swollen chunk of scar-tissue which she unconsciously covers with her hand.

'Sometimes he bashes me with an iron crowbar,' she informs me, laughing recklessly and swallowing down more beer.

When she was fourteen she used to say to me, 'What have I got to look forward to? Getting drunk and being beaten up every night.'

Well, she was right.

I leave her to meet up with some acquaintances at the Sheraton Hotel. We play tennis and afterwards sit around the pool, sipping gin. Disembodied heads speaking German float on the bubbling jacuzzi. Twilight makes everything glow unearthly pink. Great globular stars appear, unnaturally bright. I keep thinking of M's top lip as the conversation moves from Bakhtin to song-cycles to Western Desert painters to Dante to deep structure. A European film-maker insists that when a people can no longer speak their own language they cannot be said to have a culture. I resist the urge to strike him.

Afterwards we go to the Casino, just for a look. Men in cowboy hats are losing money in a desultory kind of way. As we leave we are almost run down by a black American with reflector sunglasses. He drives a white Bentley with tinted windows.

It is easy to forget that, because of the US installation at Pine Gap, Alice is a CIA town.

I am at a party of 'white advisers'. (Alice now has the highest percentage per capita of tertiary educated people in Australia, and the highest membership per capita of the Communist Party. They are all here this evening.) I know very few of them but I recognise the rhetoric. It hasn't changed in ten years. Us–them. Good guys–bad guys. The difference now is that 'bad guys' may be found in other pro-Aboriginal factions.

Alice is a small pond and socially sanctioned views are rarely challenged. Conversations seldom escape the arena of organisational politics. I wander about feeling vaguely uncomfortable and out of place, until I spy an old pal who used to work for the Central Land Council during its formative years. He is in town briefly, assisting in the Royal Commission into Aboriginal deaths in custody. He is depressed. He, too, finds Alice unrecognisable. He says, 'I just wish I knew if it were *really* any better.'

'Of course it's better. People have houses to live in and they aren't being regularly beaten by police. Turn on a television and you can see a black presenter; turn on the radio and you can hear Aboriginal languages . . .'

Neither of us is convinced.

I can see that my friend J. needs rescuing from two Californian women. They have been in town for one day and they would like to meet some shamans for a quick fix (painless, please) of Aboriginal mysticism. J. is being infinitely polite, as is her wont, but when I catch her glance she raises her eyes to heaven. New Age is the latest brand of visitor wanting instant information and access to Aboriginal people. Long-term residents like J. bear the brunt of this. When she tries to explain that things aren't quite so simple, the women assume she is being deliberately obstructive. J. has been working eighteen hours a day for the last few weeks and is fast approaching burnout, a common ailment among people working for Aboriginal organisations. I am angry on her behalf. The women flounce off, looking for more 'authentic' informants.

Another conversation forms around me. A friend's book is being discussed. Angrily. I shrink down into my seat. I introduced him to people here—they became thinly disguised characters in his novel. He is my friend and I admire his work, but these are my friends too and they feel betrayed.

Writers have never been popular here. They cause trouble. They tend not to understand the complexities of Alice's Byzantine politics and therefore the need to keep their traps shut about certain embarrassing anomalies, and, if everything else in the town has changed, the fact that its ethos is political has not.

This book has confirmed everyone's suspicions: that writers are untrustworthy. They come for a month, exploit hospitality, then misrepresent the people who opened their hearts and their filing cabinets to them.

I, too, am a writer. I think, 'Only a piece of me belongs here. The rest of me is scattered around the world, in London, New York, Sydney, inhabiting realities antagonistic to each other, suspicious of each other.'

I am in a tiny aeroplane, as substantial as cardboard, bumping along the heatwaves seven thousand feet above the desert, which looks like a Papunya-tula dot-dot painting. Pointillist background with ochre circles and patches of white. Half an hour ago we passed over the radomes of Pine Gap. They were weirdly beautiful, the way poisonous puffballs are beautiful. Now Punje, my pilot friend, is squinting at the horizon, looking for Ayers Rock. There it is, a little blue bump, and, to the right of it, a sheet of frosted glass fractured into swirls and snow crystal patterns of icier white. Lake Amadeus. Salt. Islands of orange sand in the middle of the lake are covered in stubble. And crisscrossing the salt/ice is a featherbone stitching of animal tracks.

'There's another one,' says Punje proudly. He is an engineer whose twin passions in life are water bores and aeroplanes. Where he can tap underground water, a family of Pitjantjatjara Aborigines can set up their own outstation away from the pressures of settlement life. Having gained freehold title of their land— thousands of square miles of it—the Pitjantjatjara are involved in a reverse diaspora. They are going 'home'.

I search the vastness below but can see nothing. Then a pinprick of light—one small corrugated iron roof at the end of a four-wheel drive track leading away to an empty horizon.

My understanding of the complexities and density of Aboriginal culture is limited indeed, but I have absorbed, over the years, a rudimentary knowledge of how different Aboriginal sense of place is. For them, the notion of home, or country, connotes utter belonging, and gives them a certitude concerning their function in the universe, which acts as a kind of ballast as they sail through the tempests of late twentieth-century existence. The deeper one can read their culture, the closer one comes to being able to imagine what it is to truly be 'at home in the world'.

I am going to see my old friend E., a Pitjantjatjara elder who made a journey with me years and years ago. The last time I visited him I surprised him. It was night and he was behind his windbreak, cooking roo on the fire. When he recognised me, he leapt up, gave a hoot of delight, grabbed both my breasts and shook them—as spontaneous a sign of welcome as he could give. I am as excited about seeing that tiny, wizened old coot again as a twelve-year-old would be about coming home from boarding school. The plane touches down on the red dirt runway and taxis up to the settlement.

Like all these Aboriginal communities, it looks like a garbage tip at the end of the universe. A dozen pre-fab houses in various states of dilapidation, a few wiltja (windbreaks) made of corrugated iron and branches, a couple of caravans. Mangy, skinny camp-dogs everywhere. One tin shed acts as store. A group of teenagers, out of their heads on petrol fumes, prowls around the outskirts. Plastic bags blow about in the wind like tumbleweed. Many of the old people are blind with trachoma, the kids have chronic ear, nose and throat infections and most are deaf. The community suffers all the diseases of poverty, poor diet and neglect.

A first-time visitor could be forgiven for thinking these people had been culturally annihilated. Certainly one would not suspect that here live a group of theologians engaged in constantly debating and interpreting the will of the Dreamings, or that despite the pressures on this community everyone in it maintains a complex kinship system fundamental to Aboriginal social structure. In other words, the surface transformations mask a deeper continuity.

I see E. squatting outside the store with a group of men. Because he is half blind, I get to within ten feet of him before he recognises me. Then it is all shoulder-clapping, reminiscence and laughter—

128

'desert woman' this, 'desert woman' that. (Such is my title down there and it is a step up, I feel, from 'camel lady'.) I have forgotten most of the Pitjantjatjara I knew, but it doesn't matter. Afterwards we go to his camp to see W., his wife—more frail, more shrunken, but as exquisite as ever. 'Larrrra,' they keep saying, which, roughly translated, means, 'Well I never, what a wondrous thing.'

Then I bring the presents over. For W., a brightly coloured skirt; for E., a Rambo knife almost as big as he is. He swaggers around with it, doubles up laughing, puts it back in its scabbard, takes it out and calls everyone over. He grabs me by the shoulders, smiles close up to my face, pats me continually on the chest with both hands. An old man who can speak a little English says, 'That proper good knife, *really* one, that one. You proper good wife.' Everyone nods solemnly. E. squeezes my thighs and announces to all present: 'Nyangatj minyma palya. Mulapa.' (This one is a fine woman. Absolutely.)

'Wife?' I say, very, very quietly.

Everyone begins to sing. Aboriginal singing can make the hair rise on the back of your neck. Minor key, a rise and fall at the beginning of the stanza then the rest chanted on one note. The rhythm is clapped out with hands or a pair of sticks. They are all looking at me, smiling. One old lady points at W. and me and says, 'Kutju' (one), then indicates E. Another comes up and strokes my chest downwards to the breasts, indicating painting-up for ceremony. I am now most anxious to understand *exactly* what is going on. Are they singing to welcome me, or simply as an expression of happiness, or—God almighty—is this the beginnings of a ceremonial marriage business? Am I to be his 'wife'?

Every whitefella who spends time with Anangu (Aboriginal people) will eventually be placed into a classificatory system, or 'skin'. It is possible within this system to have several mothers, several fathers, and everyone you know will be some kind of relative. Once you are classified your obligations to and ways of being with everyone in the community are clear. Because we travelled alone together, E. should have made me either his

129

'daughter' or his 'sister-in-law'. Naturally I am terribly flattered by this rather more powerful and intimate bond, though aware that it has as much to do with infinite supplies of Rambo knives as it does with affection.

Even so, the affection is genuine and I do not want to jeopardise my friendship with him, or with the other people here, by shaming anyone. I decide to retire to my own camp to consider tactics. My forty-five-year-old 'son' comes with me to make sure I'm all right.

I stay awake till 4 a.m., wondering how the hell I'm going to get out of this one. I am aware of the comedy of my predicament—it is as whimsical as only cross-cultural confusions can be. But I am anxious too. How should one behave in such a situation?

E. wakes me at six. 'Rarpie, Rarpie,' he whispers, shaking me gently and beaming down into my face.

We spend the day talking/miming. He is insistent that I bring my camels back down here, as well as a shirt, jumper and rifle, and then we will go for walks together to special places. His conversation breaks continually into song. I say, 'I can't come back this cold-time, but I will come back next cold-time.' (A year and a half away.) He replies, 'But I'll be dead by then,' and laughs. He is not afraid of death. He knows where he's going.

He asks me if I have any children yet. When I tell him no, he shakes his head and says, 'Tsc, tsc, ngaltutjarra' (poor thing), but there is a roguish gleam in his eye. I decide that tonight I will have a long dinner with the whitefellas.

I do so and return to my camp at about midnight. Anangu go to sleep as soon as it's dark. Everything is still. Not even dogs barking. I turn on the veranda light, roll my swag out under the stars and, hey ho, there is my 'husband' at the gate with his dogs. I go over to him and smile. 'What's up, E?'

'Nyuntu palya?' he says, sotto voce. (Are you okay?)

'Sure,' I say, 'palya.'

He nods, touches me on the shoulder and goes back to his wiltja.

130

Two days later the plane comes to take me back to Alice. I am certain I will never see this old man again. I feel a quite inordinate amount of grief.

'Tsc, tsc, ngaltutjarra Rarpie,' he says, shaking his head and smiling at the fascinating inconsistencies of these people without a Dreaming.

You are alone, a hundred miles from anything, strolling through a cleft in the earth, a tremendous split that happened eons ago. The sand on which you walk is a hundred feet beneath the surface which you can see above you, fringed by spinifex. The tear in the rock exposes a jagged line of sky, and the walls which enclose you (sometimes the space is only three feet wide and you can see very clearly how one wall would fit snugly into its opposite) are shiny red, black, orange, purple. You have to rub your hands over their cool smoothness. Fracture lines make you think of the noise this cataclysm made. There would have been no one to hear it, but you can almost hear it now. The crack of continents shrugging shoulders, turning in their sleep. You have the sensation of being the last, or the first person on the planet.

You walk for a mile through the fissure, and come out into open desert and a wide, white riverbed. Sudden heat, like an oven door opening in your face. Another half-mile and you reach a waterhole shaded by coolibahs. There is an obscene abundance of wildlife, which you scare away. The water is like silk on your skin; it tastes good. A few galahs stare down at you before shouting obscenities, laughing and flying off.

You head back across the hills, picking your way cautiously through thickets of daisies and solanums—white, pink, blue stars. There are snakes' tracks everywhere. When you reach the escarpment, you look a thousand feet down to the parched riverbed. In front of you is the mouth of the chasm. You notice debris in the branches of a tree beside you, but a few seconds pass before you comprehend what it means. Heaving boulders and river gums have blocked the chasm until the floodwaters rose, yes, a thousand feet. Last April this hill was drowning under a brown sea.

The scale of this place is too large, both in time and space. You do not belong here, with your insignificant lifespan and your dreams of immortality. You want to screen out the immensity, the numinousness. By the time you are back inside the furrow of rock, you are tired and very, very small.

You flop down on sand, letting the cool quiet seep in. You doze, and when you wake up you are ready to absorb detail. Beside your hand there is the husk of an iridescent green beetle whose ancestor killed the Yeperenyes. A bright orange wasp is collecting mud for its nest beside a pool of water a yard or so from your foot. Your gaze travels up slowly, over the intricate surface of rock. There is another wasp. The light is pouring down from the rip of blue sky and it forms an aura at the top of the chasm. You notice a few cobwebs up there, glazed by the sunlight. They are undulating in a breeze you cannot feel. You notice another wasp, and another, and more mats of web.

The sun is moving slowly; your gaze is absorbing more; your attention is expanding. You see, coming in waves over the lip of the chasm, through the miasma of light, thousands of wasps, and strung among all the rocks are traps of spun gold.

Your mind travels out over the surface of the desert, its blanket of spider's web, its nimbus of tiny orange wasps. You are being stretched between the incomprehensibly large and infinitesimal.

You wish there was someone to whom you could describe what you saw, because words might trap the moment and what it contained—an almost, almost belonging.

May 1989

132

STRADBROKE DREAMTIME
OODGEROO NUNUKUL

Years ago, my family — my Aboriginal family — lived on Stradbroke Island. Years before the greedy mineral seekers came to scar the landscape and break the back of this lovely island. I recall how we used to make the trip to Point Lookout. My father would saddle our horses at earlylight and we would make our way along the shoreline, then cut inland to climb over the hills covered with flowering pines, wattles and gums. The brumbies would watch our approach from a safe distance. These wild horses never trusted man, their foe. They would nuzzle their foals, warning them to stay away from their enemy.

Kath Walker (Oodgeroo Nunukul) spent her childhood with her family on Stradbroke Island, off the Queensland coast. The first half of this book, 'Stories from Stradbroke', describes episodes from her childhood days — some happy, some sad — and gives a memorable impression of Aboriginal life on the island and of a family proud of its Aboriginal heritage. The second part of the book, 'Stories from the Old and New Dreamtime', is made up of Aboriginal folklore which the author recalls hearing as a child, and of new stories written in traditional Aboriginal forms.

'Always vigorous, and deeply committed.'
OXFORD COMPANION TO AUSTRALIAN LITERATURE